# Secrets in the Cellar

The North End Mysteries Book 2

Priscilla Baker

Cover Design by
http://www.StunningBookCovers.com

*For Ben, my biggest fan*

# Chapter 1

"He still hasn't called?"

Lucy Moretti looked up as her best friend, Ally Pope, leaned through the doorway to their shared office, a tiny room located in the back of the kitchen at Alba, the restaurant Lucy owned and operated with the help of her best friend, Ally. Alba served homestyle Italian food in Boston's historic North End neighborhood, which was packed with restaurants, bakeries, historical sites—and tourists.

"Nope," Lucy responded. "I'm not sure he will at this point. It's been almost a week," she added with a sigh.

"I'm sorry, Luce," Ally responded. "That's a bummer. Have you tried calling him?"

"I did today. It went straight to voicemail," Lucy replied, raking her hand through her wavy brown hair. They were talking about Lucy's recent date with police officer Charlie Fitz, who had helped to solve the murder of one of their employees. He and Lucy had spent a very nice evening together, first visiting a Thai restaurant in downtown Boston and then taking a nice stroll along the water. When Charlie and Lucy parted ways, he had promised to call, but Lucy still hadn't heard anything.

"Well, shoot," said Ally, coming into the office and sitting down at her desk, which was really just a table shoved into the back half of the room. Lucy and Ally both had computers set up on it, side by side.

"Oh well," Lucy said with a shrug. *I do wish he'd called, though*, she thought to herself. "On to bigger and better things. How's it looking out front?" she asked her friend.

"All good, everything's under control. Quiet night out there," Ally replied, referring to the dining room. Even though she was the executive chef at the restaurant, she liked to poke her head out into the seating area every once in a while and check on things. Plus, people were always impressed when the petite woman with blonde curls introduced herself as "Chef."

It was a Tuesday night, and Lucy was focusing on getting caught up on her work. The restaurant was closed on Mondays, so Tuesdays were always kind of a "catch-up" day for Lucy. She and Ally had spent their day off yesterday in Lucy's apartment above the restaurant, perfecting a recipe for pasta agnolotti stuffed with a filling made from spring peas, goat cheese and sage.

"Have you eaten yet?" Ally asked, breaking into Lucy's thoughts. "I was going to heat up some of that leftover gnocchi from the weekend special. Do you want any?" She raised an eyebrow at her friend.

"Absolutely!" Lucy declared. "Thank you. With vodka sauce?" she asked hopefully.

"Oh fine, with vodka sauce!" Ally conceded. Lucy's love of Ally's vodka sauce was well-known in the kitchen. "Give me twenty minutes," Ally said, rising from her chair and leaving the office.

"You're the best!" Lucy called after her.

"I know!" came Ally's faint reply, drifting through the loud sounds of the kitchen. It was always noisy; with pans clanging and requests being shouted back and forth between the cooks. There was almost always music playing in the background, as well; tonight it was heavy metal. *Those guys have something new every night,* Lucy thought to herself, hearing the music.

While she waited, Lucy turned back to the financial spreadsheets pulled up on her computer screen, tuning out the loud noises coming through the doorway. The restaurant was doing well, but it was always a struggle balancing Ally's requests for the best ingredients with the need to, well, pay everybody. *If Ally had her way, she would even cancel the electricity to have just a little bit more to spend on food,* Lucy thought to herself with a smile.

They were lucky to have Ally at Alba. Before coming to Boston to take the executive chef position, she had been the sous chef at a Michelin-starred restaurant in New York City. After she and Lucy had shared a college graduation, Ally had spent the first part of her twenties working in kitchens up and down the east coast. They had met as roommates at Johnson & Wales University, in Providence, Rhode Island, where Ally had earned a degree in the culinary arts and Lucy one in hospitality management.

Lucy had been thrilled to hire Ally. Together, they had big plans for Alba. Admittedly, Lucy had struggled before Ally's arrival. She'd gone through a few executive chefs, none lasting longer than a year. But then Ally had arrived, and things changed for the better. Ally had brought a more modern flair to the food they were serving at Alba, and most definitely a stronger approach to discipline in the kitchen. She had whipped the kitchen into shape, and Lucy couldn't be more grateful.

*I should probably go check on things out front while Ally makes us dinner,* Lucy thought to herself. She rose from her chair and headed out the office door, closing it tightly behind her. Turning to the right, she headed down the narrow hallway that lined the back wall of the kitchen, towards the swinging door and the bustling dining room. Lucy paused before heading out, smoothing back her chocolate colored hair and making sure her light green blouse was pulled down neatly over her black slacks.

Taking a breath, Lucy emerged through the swinging door, taking in the sight of the dining room in front of her. About half of the tables were occupied, and servers dressed in black and white were weaving their way through the closely packed tables topped with white linen. The bartenders were expertly mixing drinks, flirting just enough with the guests at the bar to raise their tips. The wooden parquet floors practically sparkled in the low light, and open windows let in just enough of a breeze to keep the votives on the tables flickering. All in all, the dining room held all the marks of a good night.

Lucy stepped to the side, out of the way of the door, and watched the action. She liked to station herself in the dining room sometimes and just take it all in. She was always a little surprised that all this was hers.

After a moment, she stepped out into the fray, greeting the customers she recognized and introducing herself to the ones she didn't. Her father had claimed that was the secret to the success of Alba; if the customers knew your name, they always came back. And so Lucy made connections with customers, remembered their kids' names and where they lived, and so, business continued to grow.

After making the rounds, Lucy returned to the kitchen office, where she encountered Ally setting down a beautiful looking bowl of potato gnocchi with bright pink sauce, topped with a sprinkle of shredded parmesan and a pinch of sliced basil.

"You didn't have to bother plating it up so nicely for me, Ally!" Lucy exclaimed when she saw it. "But thank you. It looks gorgeous," she added gratefully.

"Oh please. There's no point eating it if it doesn't look pretty," Ally retorted jokingly as she sank into her chair. She had her own bowl of gnocchi in front of her, and the small room was filled with the delicious, spicy scent of the meal.

"Yeah, that's your philosophy. Mine is that there's no point eating it if it doesn't taste delicious," Lucy replied. "But luckily, this is both!" she said, sitting down and picking up the fork Ally had left beside the bowl, then taking an appreciative sniff.

"My pleasure," Ally replied, with an odd note in her voice. She had one hand on her computer mouse and was checking her email, with the other holding still holding her fork.

"Is everything alright?" Lucy asked her friend, concerned. Ally didn't usually concentrate so hard on emails. In fact, she rarely read them in the first place.

"Yeah, everything is fine." Ally began, speaking slowly. "It's just, well, I got this email, and I guess I was nominated for the Outstanding Young Chef award, from the American Restaurant Association," she continued, turning to face Lucy. She still held her fork, a forgotten gnocchi speared on the tines.

"Oh wow, Ally! That's fantastic!" Lucy cried out excitedly, a smile spread across her face."Congratulations! I'm really proud of you. Do you know who nominated you?" she asked eagerly.

"No, it doesn't say," Ally replied. "It wasn't you, right?" she asked Lucy hesitantly.

"No, I hate to say, it wasn't me," Lucy replied regretfully. "I wish I had thought of it, though, because you deserve it. When is the winner announced?" she asked, trying to focus on Ally as the spicy, tomato-y scent of the vodka sauce distracted her.

"The winner isn't announced until October, at a special ceremony," Ally replied. "But next week, they're announcing the finalists, who will all get to go to Charleston for the ceremony and a full week of 'special events'," she continued, reading from the email. "Charleston! I'd love to go back and visit," she added longingly. Ally had spent just over a year in Charleston, South Carolina, after graduation. Lucy felt a pang of jealousy; as much as she loved Alba, she had always held just a tiny bit of regret that after college, she had come right back to the building she'd grown up in.

"You deserve it, Al," Lucy congratulated her friend as she finally picked up the fork to take her first bite of gnocchi. "I really hope you get to go," she added, trying not to let any of the jealousy that had sprung to life inside her sneak into her voice. *Man, wouldn't it be great if there was an award for the people who owned the restaurants?* she wondered as she ate. *We work just as hard as anyone else, if not harder.*

# Chapter 2

Lucy woke with a start the next morning as a truck on the street outside honked, loud and low. *Ugh*, she groaned internally. *Why can't the rest of the world stay quiet until noon?* She glanced over at the clock and saw that it was just after eleven in the morning. She was lying in her bed, in the small apartment she had grown up in located directly over Alba. It had two small bedrooms, a living room, and a tiny kitchen. Not that Lucy ever used it, most of her meals were pilfered from the restaurant and eaten in her office downstairs.

*At least I still have some time,* she thought. *I don't have to be downstairs until three.* Since Alba only served dinner, not lunch, no one came in for work before early afternoon—except Ally, who often showed up first thing in the morning and used the empty kitchen to experiment with new dishes.

Lucy rolled out of bed and headed into the kitchen, switching on her coffee maker. She hopped in the shower while she waited for the coffee to brew.

*Today should be an easy day,* she thought as she shampooed her hair. *Weekdays are never that busy. I'll hang out up here for a little bit and straighten up before I go down to the restaurant.* It seemed like Lucy never had quite enough time in the day to get everything done, and keeping the apartment neat and tidy definitely took a backseat to the restaurant.

Finishing up her shower, Lucy threw on some sweatpants and a light sweater before wrapping herself in her old, plaid robe and heading out to the kitchen, where she poured the fresh coffee into her favorite mug before settling down on the couch. A morning person, she was not.

*Buzz!* A noise broke through Lucy's reverie—the sound of her cell phone vibrating as she received a text. She went back into the bedroom and grabbed it from where she had left it on the nightstand last night. The text was from Ally.

*Sorry for the wakeup call. Left my keys at home. Can you let me in?* the message read.

"Oh, Ally." Lucy sighed. *On my way down,* she texted back. She headed to the front door, pausing to exchange her robe for a jacket and slip on her shoes. She stepped out her door and onto the small balcony overlooking the alley behind the restaurant and the back door to the kitchen. There was a flight of wooden stairs leading down to the ground. Down below, Ally was waving at her, with a grimace on her face.

"I'm sorry!" Ally called.

"No worries," said Lucy. "The air is nice and fresh out here! And cold!" she called out as she shivered, the breeze chilling her still-wet hair.

"Oh please, it's almost summer. It's not cold, you're just a baby!" Ally teased from the bottom of the stairs, grinning.

"Wait a sec, do you hear something?" Lucy asked, pausing as a new noise caught her attention. She rested her arms on the railing of the balcony, listening intently.

"Nah, you're imagining things. Too early in the morning for you!" Ally called as she gestured for Lucy to toss down the keys.

"I definitely hear something…like a squeaking noise? Check under the stairs!" Lucy called again as she tossed the keys over the edge. Ally deftly caught them and moved towards Alba's back door.

"No way!" Ally replied as she unlocked the door. "Check yourself. I have work to do!" she called back over her shoulder as she headed into the restaurant, leaving the door cracked behind her.

*It's probably nothing,* Lucy thought to herself as she peered over the edge of the balcony. *It really is chilly out here.*

As she stood on the tiny balcony, she heard the noise again, louder this time. *Well, a quick peek can't hurt,* she thought as she headed down the stairs, pulling her jacket tighter around herself. Reaching the bottom, she ducked under the open side of the space underneath the staircase, moving aside the pile of junk that had somehow accumulated over the years.

*Why are there so many tarps under here?* she thought to herself as she kicked them aside, searching for anything out of the ordinary. Suddenly, a shape moved in the corner. *Oh no, it's a rat!* Lucy thought as she jumped back, almost slipping on the pile of tarps.

The shape came out of the corner, materializing into something that definitely wasn't a rat. *It's a kitten,* Lucy realized. *That's almost worse than a rat.*

"Ally!" she called out anxiously. "Come back out here!" she called pleadingly.

A second later Ally reappeared from the kitchen door, having exchanged her blue sweatshirt for her white chef's coat and an apron. Her blonde curls were neatly pulled back. "What's wrong?" she asked, still tucking a curl up under her flat black cap.

"It's a cat—a kitten. Under the stairs. What do I do?" Lucy called out from where she was, still standing on the pile of tarps.

"Is it alone?" Ally asked, a note of amusement in her voice.

Lucy peered under the stairs, looking for any other movement. "I think so. I don't see anything else," she responded.

"Well, then pick it up!" Ally called out, leaning against the door jamb.

"How?" Lucy asked flatly. Her family had definitely not been a pet family when she was growing up—the restaurant had been more than enough to keep them busy.

"What do you mean, how? Just pick it up! With your hands!" Ally called back, laughter in her voice.

Lucy grimaced and moved to where the kitten was, just sitting and staring at her. She reached out, expecting the animal to back into the corner, but it just looked at her before meowing loudly.

"It made a noise! What does that mean?" Lucy called out worriedly.

"Cats meow sometimes, Luce! Just pick it up, you can't leave it there!" Ally replied, coming closer.

Lucy reached forward and grabbed the kitten, pulling it towards her and stepping out from under the stairs triumphantly with her arms outstretched.

Ally laughed. "What are you doing? Have you ever seen a cat before? That's not how you hold it!" The tiny creature meowed again, a high-pitched squeak, as if to echo Ally's point.

"Then fine, you take it!" Lucy replied, pointing the cat at her friend. "Besides, no, I'm actually not sure if I've ever seen a kitten before in real life, thank you very much. Not many people in the city have pets," she pointed out to her friend, who had grown up in the classic suburban lifestyle, which included cats and dogs, and even a rabbit, in Ally's case.

"No way am I taking that thing! I'll get fur all over my jacket, and this is the last clean one," Ally said, gesturing at her spotless white coat. "Besides, finders keepers. That thing is yours now!" Ally laughed.

"What do I do with it?" Lucy asked, peering at the kitten more closely in the daylight. It was a brown tabby with white feet and a white spot on the tip of its tail, it's fur damp and matted. It peered back at her with big brown eyes. It was so light, Lucy almost felt like she wasn't holding anything at all.

"Take it upstairs! You certainly can't bring it in here," Ally said, stepping back inside the kitchen. "The health inspector would have a fit. Bring it up to the apartment and give it some water. I can bring up a little bit of salmon—we have plenty. Find a blanket or something for it." Ally commanded, letting the kitchen door close behind her as she disappeared into the kitchen.

"Well, alright then, cat," Lucy said to the kitten in her arms. "I guess we're going upstairs. Ally says."

She headed back upstairs, still uncertain as to why Ally had laughed at her cat-holding technique. The door was still open, and she headed right inside, leaving the door cracked for Ally.

Heading directly to the bathroom, Lucy put the cat down on the bathmat. It immediately flopped over and started purring, still staring at her with dark, expectant eyes.

"Don't get too comfy here, cat," she warned. "There's no way you're staying. I'll find someone who knows how to hold a cat, and you can go live with them," she added. She stepped backwards out of the bathroom, closing the door tightly behind her.

In the kitchen, Lucy searched through the cabinets, looking for something she could use as a water dish for the cat. In the back of the upper cabinet over the fridge, she finally spied a little pink bowl. *Oh wow,* she thought. *I'm pretty sure that was mine, way back when. Mom and Dad really knew how to hang on to things.* By standing on her tiptoes, she could just barely reach it.

She gave the little bowl a quick rinse in the sink before filling it up and carefully carrying it over to the bathroom. "Watch out, kitty!" she called out as she pushed the door open. The little cat was still on the bathmat, lounging on it's side, in the exact same place where she'd left it.

"Do you want some water?" she asked it, setting the bowl down on the floor. The cat looked at it, but didn't make a move. "Are you hungry, then?" she asked. "Don't worry, Ally will be here soon," she told it, using two fingers to pat the cat awkwardly on the top of its head.

They sat there, staring at each other, until Lucy heard the front door of the apartment creak open. "Ally?" she called out. "We're in the bathroom."

The bathroom door opened behind them as Ally entered the small room.

"Why are you both in here?" Ally asked. "Were you two just having a staring contest?"

"Well, I don't want it in the rest of my apartment! It has so much hair—and probably fleas too!" Lucy replied indignantly. "It can stay in here until I find someone who wants it. This bathroom is very comfortable," she added jokingly, gesturing to the tiny room. Even sitting on the floor as they were, the room barely fit both women and the tiny cat.

Ally reached out to pet the cat, running her hand down its back. She put down a small plate from the restaurant with a little bit of leftover salmon from the night before on it. The cat eagerly sat up and started eating the fish.

Both women sat, watching the cat eat. "So, have you heard anything about the Outstanding Young Chef award? Lucy asked casually.

"No, nothing," Ally replied. "I did do some research, though. Apparently a bunch of chefs who've won have gone on to be famous," she said, looking at the ground while she absentmindedly played with the hem of her white coat.

"What, like on TV?" Lucy asked her friend.

"No, like really famous. Winning fancier awards, writing cookbooks, teaching at places like the Culinary Institute of America, things like that," Ally said. "I don't know, sometimes I think something like that would be pretty cool," she continued, shrugging.

"You'd leave us behind for all that?" Lucy joked, trying to hide the tinge of disappointment in her voice. She'd hired Ally after a long string of chefs that hadn't worked out, and had been excited to have someone who seemed to be on board for the long haul. Ally had certainly been talking like she planned on sticking around, the two of them were making all sorts of plans for the next few years.

"I'll have to at some point," Ally protested, finally looking up to meet Lucy's eyes. "Do you still want to be working long hours like this, spending so much time on your feet, not having any personal life, when you're fifty?" she asked.

"That's my plan," Lucy replied. "My grandparents and my parents both did it, why not me?" she asked rhetorically.

"Well, I want something more than that someday. And I'm going to grab every chance I can to get there," Ally said, looking directly at her friend.

They both drifted awkwardly into silence, watching as the kitten finished its salmon and took a long drink of water. "What now?" Lucy asked.

"Well," said Ally, "it's going to have to go to the bathroom eventually. You probably want to prepare for that."

"Oh," replied Lucy, hesitantly. "How do I do that?" she asked, afraid of what the answer might be.

"Well, it's a stray, so definitely not litter-box trained. Not that you have a box, anyway," Ally said. "Honestly, I would just get some newspaper and put it on the floor. That way you can just replace it as needed. It looks like it's a boy, so you probably want to just cover the whole floor. They're usually a little messier," Ally continued.

"How do you know all this?" Lucy asked.

"How do I know how to hold a cat, and what to feed it?" Ally laughed. "It's not hard. I mean, my family always had cats when I was growing up."

"Do you want this one?" Lucy asked her friend hopefully. "Or maybe your parents want it?" she added.

"Ha!" Ally chortled. "Of course not. Not only am I not allowed to have pets, my apartment is so small I would probably step on it. And my parents vowed that after the kids were out of the house, they were done with pets. This one's all you, Luce."

"No way am I keeping this thing. I'll find someone who wants it," Lucy said confidently, using her two fingers again to pat the kitten on the top of his head. He leaned into her hand, seeming to appreciate the affection, however tentatively it was given.

"Sure, definitely," Ally replied skeptically. "In the meantime, though, you should head down to the corner store and get some newspaper so this poor baby can go to the bathroom," Ally said, standing up and reopening the bathroom door. She stepped out of the bathroom and stretched, her back letting out a loud *crack.* "Ugh. I am way too old to be spending time sitting on the floor," she groaned.

"Well then come on!" Lucy urged her friend. "A walk will shake things out," she added hopefully.

"No, I have to get back to the kitchen," Ally said quickly. "I have the ovens preheating. Just head down to Rafael's place and get a few copies of today's newspaper. Cover the whole floor with it," she instructed, leaving the small apartment and heading down the stairs before Lucy could even reply.

"Well, kitty, I guess we're on our own," Lucy told the tiny kitten, staring back at her through the cracked bathroom door. "I'll be back soon," she promised it before closing the door.

# Chapter 3

"Lucy, is it true?" one of the cooks, Chris, called out as he saw Lucy walking past his station, where he was slicing vegetables. It was evening now— Lucy had spent the day kitten-proofing the bathroom of her apartment after Ally had returned to the restaurant.

"Is what true?" Lucy asked.

"Do you really have a cat now?" he asked, smiling.

"No, I do not!" Lucy cried indignantly. "I am temporarily housing a kitten while I find someone who can take it. Do you want it?" she offered.

"No way! My wife would kill me," Chris said with a laugh. "How old is it?" he asked curiously.

"Actually, I have no idea," Lucy replied. "It's pretty small, so it must be young. It's super hungry though—it ate half of a salmon steak," she told him.

"Damn, that cat eats better than I do," Chris commented, laughing.

"Isn't that the truth!" Lucy replied, moving past his station to head out into the dining room. One of the servers, Mary, was having trouble with the computer that sent orders from the front of the house to the back. Somehow, Lucy had gained a reputation as the one who knew how to fix it—really, she was the only one patient enough to coax it back to life.

She emerged into the dining room and turned into the small wait station. Mary was there, fiddling with the screen, her pale face practically glowing in the green-tinged light from the screen. "Thanks, Lucy," she said, stepping aside. "It's frozen again."

"Oh, great." Lucy groaned. "Okay, I'll get to work on it. Make sure all the servers are telling Ally their orders. Don't let any tables fall behind while I get this fixed," she directed. Mary had stepped into the unofficial 'head server' role that Donovan Fagan had left behind when he was killed earlier in the year.

"I'm on it. Good luck," Mary added as she left Lucy alone in the tiny wait station. It was at the back of the dining room, located right next to the bar with a wall between them. It was where the computer for placing orders was, as well as the extra place settings, salt and pepper shakers, anything the servers might need to keep things running smoothly and make sure everyone had a good experience.

"Alright, it's just me and you now, old friend," Lucy muttered to the computer, feeling like she was preparing for battle.

She started with all the usual tricks—hitting the small reset button on the back, hitting the larger power button next to it. Lucy did her best to stifle a groan of frustration - nothing seemed to work. The machine's screen saver, a maniacal-looking cartoon crab, was just staring back at her, bouncing from corner to corner on the screen. "Alright, fine," Lucy said to the machine as she got down on her hands and knees. Unplugging the computer meant crawling under the cabinet it was stored on—a prospect Lucy never relished.

Squeezing up against the cabinet, her arm stretched as far as it would go, Lucy could just barely reach the plug. "Ha!" she whispered triumphantly as she tugged it out of the wall and waited. It made a satisfying *clunk* as the hefty plug hit the wooden floor. The next part, plugging it back in without the benefit of a line of sight, was always trickier. After a moment, she started feeling around, trying to get the plug back in.

*It always takes a minute,* she thought to herself. Finally, the plug caught on one of the holes in the outlet and slid back into the wall. She extricated herself from under the cabinet and stood back up, smoothing down the aqua-colored blouse she was wearing. *Hope nobody saw any of that,* she thought, exhaling forcefully to clear the dust out of her nose. She turned around, back towards the dining room, only to notice a little boy, maybe five or six, watching her intently. He was seated with several adults at the table nearest to the wait station, and they were all ignoring him completely. When he saw that she had turned around, the bored expression on his face started to transform into a smile.

While she waited for the computer to reboot, Lucy made her way over to the table. "Hi, folks," she greeted them, pasting a big smile on her face. "I'm sorry to interrupt, but I just wanted to check and see how everything is tonight. Are you enjoying the food?" she asked.

"Yes, we most certainly are!" the tall man seated next to the boy answered for the group.

"Can I get you anything else? Another bottle of wine?" Lucy offered, gesturing to the nearly empty bottle of house red sitting in the center of their table.

The man looked around the table, collecting nods from the group, and then replied, "Sure, why not?" with a laugh.

"Of course, sir," Lucy replied before directing her attention to the little boy. "And how about you, young man?" she asked. "I happen to have some crayons and a few coloring pages—would you like me to bring some over while you wait for your food?"

His small smile grew larger. "Yes!" he answered excitedly, bouncing up and down in his chair.

"Robert, what do you say?" the tall man prodded him with a smile, stilling the boy by laying a hand on his shoulder.

"Thank you, ma'am!" Robert replied politely, his grin betraying his excitement.

"My pleasure!" Lucy told him, returning his smile as she moved away to collect the wine from the bar and the crayons from the host stand.

She encountered Mary near the front door of the restaurant, where she had been chatting with the host, and handed the items over. "Mary, would you mind dropping these off at table ten, with the little boy?" Lucy asked. "I don't have a wine key, so I need you to open the bottle."

"No problem," Mary said, taking the items. "That boy is a sweetheart, isn't he?" she commented. "He was so polite when he ordered," she added with a smile. "Is the computer all set?" she asked, changing subjects.

"It's restarting now," Lucy told her. "It should be all set, though. Usually it just needs to be unplugged and plugged back in," she explained.

"Awesome. Thanks, boss. I'll try that next time!" Mary said gratefully before turning and heading deeper into the dining room.

Lucy stood by the host stand for a moment, making small talk with Alex, the host. He was a college student in his second year, born and raised in Iowa before coming to Boston. He was a sweet kid, and Lucy always enjoyed talking to him.

"Lucy, do you think there's any chance of me getting next Saturday off?" he asked hopefully. "I have plans. Well, I hope I'll have plans," he said sheepishly.

"Of course, Alex, no problem," Lucy said, smiling. "Just write it down for me and leave it on my desk. Are you doing anything fun?" she asked.

"Well, there's this girl in my applied psychology class," Alex replied, blushing. "I'd really like to take her out to dinner."

"Say no more," Lucy replied. "I'll make sure it's taken care of," she added with a smile.

"Thanks, Lucy," he said, his tone relieved. "I really appreciate it."

"No problem—I'm looking forward to hearing all about it!" she teased him. With that, she stepped away, heading back towards the kitchen office, where her paperwork was waiting. It seemed like it never ended, when all she really wanted to do this time of night was head upstairs and have a glass of wine on her own couch.

*Oh well,* she thought to herself. *Someone has to make sure things are taken care of around here!*

Lucy headed through the swinging door, almost bumping into Ally, who was coming from the other direction. "Sorry, Al," she said with a tight smile. Things had been a little awkward between the two of them since their heart-to-heart over the kitten that morning.

Ally didn't respond, continuing towards the dining room.

"What, now that you're a hotshot award winner, you don't say 'excuse me'?" Lucy burst out without thinking.

"What did you say?" Ally shot back, turning around. "I couldn't hear you. Say that again," she challenged, coming back towards Lucy.

"You know kitchen rules as well as anyone, Ally!" exclaimed Lucy. "Behind, coming through, knife, *excuse me,*" she said, stressing the last one. "You have to communicate. Otherwise, people get hurt," she continued, trying to find a way to de-escalate the situation.

"You're right, I do know the rules," Ally declared. "And the rules say I can do anything I want. I don't have to keep working here. I can leave if I want to," she declared, anger coloring her cheeks. With that, she turned back towards the dining room.

"Ally, come on," Lucy said pleadingly. "You don't have to go anywhere," she said, changing her tone and trying to make peace. "I'm sorry," she called after her friend.

Ally kept walking. "I'm not an award winner, not yet!" she called over her shoulder, ignoring Lucy's apology. "But once I am, who

knows where that will take me?" she declared as
she moved through the swinging door.

# Chapter 4

The next morning, Lucy wrinkled her nose as she held the garbage bag out far in front of her, carefully keeping her balance as she descended the stairs from the apartment. Since she spent so little time in the apartment, taking out the trash was rarely a priority. But now, with the kitten's fragrant additions to her garbage can, it was suddenly becoming a lot more important.

"Hey, Lucy!" a voice called out from below. Lucy grimaced as she reached the bottom of the stairs and spotted her neighbor, Lucas Ricci. He owned the restaurant next door, Bella Luna. He was in the middle of renovating the restaurant, and often stopped by to ask permission for a dumpster or truck to occupy the alley for a few days. They had never gotten along as children, but their working relationship had been steady since both took over their family-owned restaurants.

"Hey, Lucas! How's the project going?" Lucy asked. Her feelings about Lucas aside, she was excited to see what Bella Luna would look like after all the work. The two restaurants had started out nearly identical, sharing a building as they did. It would be good for customers to see a difference between the two.

"It's going really well, actually. Really, really well. We actually found a safe in the basement yesterday—it had been bricked over. It was installed when my grandfather bought the building and converted it into the restaurants," Lucas replied. "And then somewhere along the way, maybe a few years later when my Grandpa finished the basement, it was covered up," he added.

"That's great," Lucy replied distractedly as she moved to the dumpster and dropped the bag inside. She brushed her hands off as she turned back around to face Lucas.

"The construction team offered to drill the safe open," Lucas continued. "Inside, I found the blueprint from when it was originally converted from a warehouse into the restaurants, back in 1938. My grandfather, Marco Ricci, is listed as the owner for both restaurants," Lucas responded, greedily rubbing his hands together.

Lucy took a step back, crossing her arms. "Well, then that must have been from before Nonno bought Alba," Lucy responded slowly, trying to figure out what direction Lucas was heading in. "If it was before Nonno bought the place, it makes perfect sense for Marco to be listed as the owner for both," she said again.

"You're right," Lucas admitted, waving a hand. "But the thing is, regardless of when Alba opened, I found paperwork that shows that Angelo Moretti stopped paying rent in 1941. His last payment was the same month that my grandfather was murdered," he said, taking a step closer to Lucy. "And Angelo never paid rent again. I'm thinking he took advantage of my grandmother and used the opportunity to stop paying rent. What I'm saying here, Lucy," Lucas continued, a menacing grin spreading over his handsome face, "is that I have proof that my family owns the entire building. Angelo Moretti never actually purchased it, and he certainly missed a lot of rent payments. We own both Bella Luna and Alba," he said firmly, one hand clenching into a fist.

"What? That can't possibly be right," Lucy declared defensively, ignoring the feeling of dread coming over her. "My grandfather owned our restaurant, and then my father, and now I do," she continued definitively. "I'd like to show my lawyer anything you have that says otherwise," she bluffed. *Do I even know any lawyers?* Lucy wondered silently.

"Go right ahead," Lucas replied, his face twisting into anger. Lucy took a step back, surprised at his sudden transformation. "And when your lawyer says that I'm right, I'll be collecting sixty years of back rent. Or, you could always pony up a few million dollars and buy the place. But more likely, I'll be expanding Bella Luna into the space currently occupied by Alba, once you're evicted," he said, taking another step closer.

"And furthermore," he continued, stepping even closer, now looming over Lucy, "I wouldn't be surprised if your grandfather was responsible for the bullet that ended up in my grandfather's back. Angelo Moretti needed to do *something* to set off his little scam on my poor grandmother," Lucas added confidently.

"What?" Lucy gasped, her fists clenching as she was overwhelmed by emotion. "How dare you!" she cried out, growing enraged. "My nonno did no such thing. Don't you dare accuse him of murder!"

"I'll see that my family gets what it should have had all along." Lucas declared, turning back towards his restaurant. "I'll bring those documents I mentioned over later," he called confidently, sounding like nothing had happened. He disappeared inside Bella Luna, the door slamming behind him. The sound echoed through the now-silent alley.

Lucy leaned back against the stair railing heading up to her apartment, feeling her shoulders slump in defeat. "What am I going to do?" she asked herself out loud as tears threatened to spill out onto her cheeks.

"Hello?" Ally's voice called out from the doorway into Alba. "Oh, it's you," she said coldly, seeing Lucy. "I heard voices. Who were you talking to?" Ally asked as she stepped outside.

"Lucas, from next door. He came by to…give me some news, I guess is how you'd put it," Lucy replied, sniffling and standing up straight. She didn't want to cry in front of Ally, not after their fight the night before.

"What's going on? Are the renovations going to take longer than they thought?" Ally asked, her voice still cold and formal.

"No, it's nothing to do with that. He managed to find a blueprint of the building from 1938, and thinks that his father still owns the entire building, Alba included," Lucy replied, stepping towards her friend. "He also accused my nonno of murder," she added, her voice cracking.

"That can't be true, right?" Ally asked, her hand rising to cover her mouth. "I mean, I never met the man, but from what I've heard, I seriously doubt that your grandfather would have murdered anyone. Who is he supposed to have killed, anyway?" Ally asked, speaking quickly. "Besides, your family has to own this building. When did Alba open? It was after 1938, right? Maybe Lucas's blueprint is just from before your grandpa bought the restaurant," she continued hopefully.

"Hold on," Lucy replied, struggling to organize her thoughts. "Actually, you might be right. I think it was 1939, but I have the original menus upstairs in the apartment. My grandparents saved the menus from the day they opened. Let me go take a look," she added, heading towards the stairs.

"I'll come with you," Ally said quickly. "Hey, Luce, I'm sorry about last night," she offered, leaving the doorway and taking a step towards her friend.

"I know. I am too. It was stupid. I was an ass," Lucy apologized. "You just didn't hear me. I shouldn't have gotten so worked up," she added, feeling like a fool for letting her jealousy infect their friendship.

"Yeah, you were an ass," Ally agreed, nodding before letting a small smile spread across her face. "Is there something wrong?" she asked. "Besides all this, I mean. It just seems like you've been off for a few days," she added.

"Nope," Lucy said, feeling bad about the white lie she was telling. *I can't make her feel bad about being nominated for this award. It's what she's been working towards for years*, Lucy realized.

"Good," Ally said firmly. "You'd tell me if there was, right?" she asked, raising an eyebrow at Lucy.

"Yes," Lucy said firmly, nodding her head. "Friends?" she asked.

"Friends," Ally agreed, hugging Lucy.

Together, they headed up the stairs, Lucy in the lead. She pushed open the door to the apartment. "Ignore the mess," she instructed Ally, waving a hand at the pile of laundry waiting to be done on top of the washing machine tucked in the corner.

"I always do!" Ally quipped. Lucy closed the door and they both sat down on the old couch in the living room, one that Lucy's grandmother had originally purchased. "Okay, tell me again what happened. Why on earth would Lucas accuse your grandpa of murdering someone?" Ally asked.

"It's all tied together. Let me just start from the beginning," Lucy said, taking a deep breath.

"Tell me exactly what he said," Ally requested, pulling her legs up onto the couch and turning to face Lucy.

"I mean, it's pretty much what I told you. He said he found a blueprint from 1938, which is after his grandfather divided the space into two restaurants, but before Alba opened. I guess maybe Marco ran both restaurants for a time, before my grandfather started renting Alba," she added as an aside.

"He said he found rent payments for the restaurant that stopped in 1941, which is when his grandfather died. He didn't say when they started. Anyway, Marco Ricci was murdered, right outside the restaurant. His wife, Elena, found him with a bullet in his back on the sidewalk. My nonno said she never recovered from that, and she never spoke of it again" Lucy explained. "And apparently, Lucas now thinks that my grandfather is the one who killed him. 'To set off his scheme,' is how Lucas put it."

"That can't be true," Ally murmured, wrinkling her brow.

"I don't believe it for a second." Lucy declared. "It was right before World War II, and I know that this whole neighborhood, being Italian, struggled. There was a lot of prejudice against them," she told her friend, sighing. "Anyway, I guess there were no more records of rent being paid after Marco died, and he thinks that my grandfather, Angelo, took advantage of the situation and stopped paying," Lucy finished, sighing heavily.

"But how would he get away with that?" Ally asked. "Eventually, Marco's widow would have to have noticed that nobody was paying the rent for Alba. She managed to keep the restaurant running for years on her own after Marco's death. She had to have been a good businesswoman."

"I agree. That's why I think it's crap. There's no way my grandfather would do that, either scam Elena or kill Marco. And I don't think Lucas is giving his grandmother enough credit. She ran a business for decades; she would have known if someone wasn't paying her what she was due," Lucy answered, pushing herself up off the couch. "Come on, let's go try to find those menus and make sure of the opening date. I'm guessing they're in the spare room, there are a ton of old papers in there," she told her friend.

"I've never heard you call your grandfather Nonno before," Ally commented as they moved across the tiny apartment. "Is that what you called him?" she asked curiously.

"Yeah," Lucy replied distractedly, stepping into the spare room. "My Nonno and Nonna. Italian, you know. They spoke a lot of it around the restaurant," she added.

"That's sweet," Ally said. "It's nice to hear you talk about them like this," she continued with a smile. "Even if it did take Lucas accusing your nonno of murder to set it off," she added sarcastically.

The spare room, which had been Lucy's childhood bedroom, and her father's before that, was packed full of detritus from the restaurant that had accumulated over the years. Spare tables and chairs, boxes of glasses and silverware, even extra parts for the equipment. Once Lucy had moved into the larger bedroom after her parents retired, this one had turned into a storage space.

Under the far window, which looked down on Salem Street over the front door of the restaurant, rested an old trunk, one that had traveled with Angelo and Rosa Moretti from Italy. It was made of deep red leather, with a hinged lid and stickers from the ship that had transported them pasted on its sides. "I think we should start with that," Lucy said, gesturing towards it. "That's where they kept the most important things. That trunk came with them from the old country," she told Ally, smiling at the phrase her nonno had loved to use.

"Let's do it," Ally agreed, crossing the room and pulling the trunk away from the wall. She had to strain to do so, the trunk was almost as big as she was. Together, Lucy and Ally lifted the lid, resting it against the wall. Inside were stacks of papers and photo albums, some going back to when Marco and Rosa were first married in Italy. There was a black-and-white photograph tucked into the lining of the lid, only half of it showing. Lucy carefully slid it out, revealing a group of laughing teens against the backdrop of an Italian village. Lucy carefully flipped it over to read the back.

"Look," she said, tilting the picture so Ally could see. "This is from before they were married. It says it was taken in 1930, and they were married in 1932." Lucy paused for a second, taking in the image of her grandparents as carefree teenagers in their homeland, before all the stress and anxiety of life had begun for them.

"That's incredible," Ally replied, speaking softly. "You're so lucky to have such a connection to your grandparents, and to have pictures like this. I hardly knew mine at all." She sighed.

"To be fair, I'm not that close with my maternal grandparents," Lucy replied. "They're still alive, out on the west coast in Washington state. That's why my parents moved out west after they retired, to be closer to them. I haven't seen any of them in years," she said, a note of regret sneaking into her voice.

"Well, you'll have to plan a trip! You've been an east coast girl all your life—time to live a little!" Ally replied, poking her friend in the side with an elbow.

"Ow! No way. You want me to leave you alone with these jackals?" Lucy asked, gesturing towards the floor at the restaurant below.

"Nope! Not even a little bit," Ally replied, laughing.

"Good! Now let's focus. Do you see those menus in here?" Lucy asked, moving aside some of the picture albums in the trunk.

"Let me sort through this stack," Ally offered, collecting some of the loose papers into a pile. "Do you want to keep looking through the albums? Maybe they have one for the restaurant," she continued hopefully.

Ally and Lucy sat in silence for a few minutes, pausing in their work occasionally to show the other something interesting they had found. They started a pile of old pictures and memorabilia from the restaurant, although they didn't find the menus they were looking for.

"I think maybe it's time to spruce up some of the decor down in the dining room," Lucy said. "Could we use some of this?" she wondered.

"Lucy, that is a magnificent idea," Ally declared. "How cool would that be? I mean, look at this—here are your grandfather's handwritten recipes for things that are still on the menu. I think the customers would love that!" she said enthusiastically.

"I agree! Let's set those things aside. Maybe we can do some sort of display near the window," Lucy suggested. "Anyway, are you getting hungry?" she asked her friend, changing the subject. "I'm pretty sure Lucas can hear my stomach growling from next door," she continued with a laugh.

"I could definitely eat. Do you actually have any food up here?" Ally said. "I could run down to the restaurant and whip something up," she offered.

"I have those agnolotti we made on Monday," Lucy said. "I stuck the leftovers in the freezer. Do you want to do that?"

"Definitely! Those were delicious!" Ally cried, jumping up and doing a quick stretch. "Give me a few minutes. Oh, I can make a sauce too," she muttered to herself as she bustled out of the small room.

"Let me know if I can help!" Lucy called after her, laughing as she watched her friend disappear through the doorway. She kept sorting through the piles of documents and photographs, even finding an old chef coat, neatly folded, that had belonged to her grandfather. It was still starched stiff, even after all these years. Lucy smiled to herself as she gently rubbed her finger over his name embroidered on the right breast. *I won't let Lucas Ricci take this place, Nonno,* she promised silently.

A short while later, Ally's voice rang out from the kitchen, breaking into Lucy's racing thoughts. "Come and get it!" she called. Lucy hopped up, careful not to disturb the piles she had surrounded herself with. She made her way out to the kitchen, where Ally was setting down two bowls on the counter in front of the bar stools. Living in such a small apartment, that was the closest thing Lucy had to a table.

"I used some of your cream," Ally said. "And I ran down to the restaurant too—I made this really light cream tarragon sauce I used to do at the restaurant in New York. I think you'll like it with the agnolotti," she continued, plopping down a fork next to the bowl.

The agnolotti were stuffed with a creamy blend of fresh peas, goat cheese and just a hint of sage. Topped with the sauce, they looked very tempting. Ally came around the counter and sat down next to Lucy. "Well, dig in!" she said enthusiastically, picking up her fork.

Lucy speared one of the pasta pouches on her fork and took a bite, savoring the flavors as they filled her mouth. The tart, creamy goat cheese worked well with the sweetness of the peas and the flavors of the herbs.

"Ally," she said, her mouth still full, "this *has* to go on the menu. This is amazing!" she continued, swallowing and then stuffing another bite into her mouth.

"You think?" Ally asked, carefully taking a small bite. "Oh," she said after a second. "This is good."

"It's incredible," Lucy said. "The sauce really kicks it up a notch. It's going on the menu. Write up the recipe and we'll do it next week," she said decisively.

"Give me two weeks!" Ally protested, scooping up another agnolotti onto her fork. "Remember how long it took us to make this tiny little batch? We're going to need a few days to turn out enough to run it as a special," she explained quickly.

"Alright, alright," Lucy conceded. "Two weeks."

"Good," Ally said, finishing the last of her pasta, carefully using her fork to scrape up the remaining sauce in her bowl.

"Oh, that was really good," Lucy said again, leaning against the back of her chair. "Thanks, Ally. Now I feel like I can tackle the rest of those papers. Do you want to get back to searching and I'll handle the dishes?" she offered.

"That's the best thing you've said to me all day!" Ally said, laughing. She handed over her empty bowl and headed back toward the spare room they had been working in, while Lucy got started cleaning up the kitchen.

A few minutes later, Lucy joined her friend again. "Any luck?" she asked, sinking down onto the floor.

"Not yet," Ally replied, pulling a fresh stack of albums out of the trunk. "Here, do you want to start looking through this?" she asked, handing it to Lucy.

"Sure thing," Lucy replied, carefully taking the stack and setting it down next to her.

"Wait, what's this?" Lucy said, gently pulling a sheet of paper out of a photo album. Across the top, in an old-fashioned typeface, it read, "Alba: Opening Day," and underneath that, in smaller letters, "April 1939."

"This is it!" Lucy exclaimed. "So, the restaurant definitely opened in 1939, and my grandfather paid rent to Marco Ricci through 1941. But what happened after that?" she wondered, absentmindedly tracing her fingers over the word "Alba" on the menu.

"That is the million-dollar question," Ally replied. "Maybe literally. Do you have any idea how much money he wants in back rent?" she asked.

"Nope," Lucy said. "I didn't even think to ask, I was so freaked out," she admitted. "I also told him I have a lawyer, which was a total lie. I don't even know how you get a lawyer," she joked weakly.

"Well, that was good thinking, at least!" Ally replied enthusiastically. Ally was good at always seeing the positive in the situation. "I have a friend who's a lawyer," she volunteered. "We went to high school together, and now he lives here in the city. I don't know what kind of lawyer, but hopefully he can help, or at least recommend someone," she continued.

"Oh Ally, that would be wonderful. Thank you. Can I have his number?" Lucy asked. "I feel like I should get a lawyer as soon as I can," she added ruefully.

"Let's call him together," Ally said, pulling out her cell phone. She was interrupted by a loud *crash* from the bathroom.

"The cat!" Lucy exclaimed, startling. "I forgot all about the cat!" She jumped to her feet and hurried across the small apartment.

"Okay," Ally called out patiently. "I'll give him a call while you make sure that poor thing is still alive," she added.

Lucy carefully opened the door to the bathroom, where she was greeted by the kitten's small face peering up at her from where he was curled up inside the sink. The toiletries she usually kept on the bathroom counter were scattered all over the bathroom floor.

"Well, that explains the noise," she said to the kitten, moving inside the bathroom and shutting the door behind her.

"What are you doing in the sink?" she asked him as she picked up her toothbrush. "You know, I had this stuff up there for a reason," she continued, gesturing at the items now scattered across the floor. "I guess maybe I didn't do a very good job kitten-proofing this room," she admitted, looking around at the destruction. All her toiletries were on the floor, her towel had been dragged from it's hook onto the floor, and the bathmat was scrunched into the corner, with a new, mysterious stain on it.

The tiny cat looked back at her with an innocent expression.

"Oh fine!" Lucy conceded. "You can have the sink. I'll put all this stuff somewhere else." She opened the door to the cabinet under the sink and shoved everything inside. "I'll deal with everything else later," she said, more to herself than to the kitten. She gave him a tentative pat on the head.

"Behave, now, please!" she said to him as she exited the bathroom.

"I talked to my friend," Ally said, sliding her phone back into her pocket as she met Lucy in the living room. "It's not his area of expertise, but he says he's happy to take a look at what Lucas has," she informed Lucy. "He says it sounds like you need to find some proof that your grandfather continued making payments, or some proof of when he actually bought the building. Do you know if any of his old records are floating around anywhere?" Ally asked.

"I'll certainly look, but I doubt it. He wasn't very good at keeping records in the first place, which is why my dad taught me to be so meticulous. He spent a lot of time untangling problems caused by my grandfather's lack of organization skills," Lucy explained to her friend.

"Well, that explains a lot!" Ally exclaimed with a grin. "You and your dad keep the best records I've ever seen."

"I do love my file folders!" Lucy responded with a laugh. "Oh well. I'll give my dad a call tomorrow. When I talked to him last week, he told me he was going on a fishing trip and wouldn't be back until then. Who knows," she said hopefully, "Maybe he'll be able to clear this whole thing up. But for now, we'd better get downstairs! It's already past four o'clock," she noted, gesturing to the clock hanging on the living room wall.

"Oh, shoot!" Ally cried. "I have sauces to make!"

# Chapter 5

The next morning found Lucy sitting on the small floral-print couch in her apartment, sipping her coffee. She was killing time until it was a reasonable hour out in Washington, where her parents lived, to call her father and share Lucas's accusations.

Dinner service had gone smoothly the night before, even if she wasn't quite able to shake the feeling of dread that Lucas's visit had brought on. She had tossed and turned all night. *I can't believe Lucas is trying to pull a stunt like this. He can't just steal the restaurant out from under us, and accuse Nonno of murder all in one breath. There has to be something, somewhere. There's no way Nonno didn't own our restaurant.* She'd had nightmares about walking through the back door of the restaurant and finding it transformed into a fast-food restaurant, with Lucas grinning his menacing smile in the corner.

Shaking herself out of her reverie, Lucy busied herself by running down to the restaurant to grab another piece of salmon for the little kitten causing a ruckus in her bathroom. She had let it out of the bathroom while she showered that morning, and it had taken her almost half an hour to find it again. She returned to the apartment and plopped the salmon into a shallow bowl.

"Here you go, kitty," she said as she cracked open the bathroom door. "I have some breakfast for you," she continued. She crouched down on the floor and reached a hand out towards the cat. "How old are you, kitty?" she asked him curiously. He ignored the question, frantically sniffing at the bowl in her hand.

"I guess I'll have to find someone who knows how to tell cat ages. Maybe Ally does," she said to the kitten as it wolfed down the raw salmon filet. Lucy refilled the water bowl and carefully replaced the newspaper she and Ally had set down as a makeshift litter box. She grabbed the bathmat with the mysterious stain and added it to the ever-growing laundry pile.

"What I really have to do, little kitty, is find someone who wants to keep you," she told the animal, returning to the bathroom. The kitten stopped eating and stared at her for a second before returning to it's meal. "Alright, alright, I'll leave you alone to eat," she conceded, leaving the bathroom and shutting the door.

Lucy moved aimlessly around the apartment, tidying up. She finally put in a load of laundry, grimacing at the scent wafting from the pile. Even though she didn't actually do any cooking, everything she wore to work managed to smell like grease. Doing laundry was always low on Lucy's priority list - she had a washing machine, but not a dryer, and so everything had to be dried on a retractable laundry line her grandfather had installed in the living room. Doing laundry was always quite an event.

*I'll need more newspaper soon for that little guy,*Lucy realized. *Plus, that will kill some more time.* Sliding on her sneakers and a light jacket, Lucy left the apartment, careful to lock the door behind her. After a break-in at the restaurant earlier that year, Lucy was always sure to lock the doors.

She headed down the steps and out onto Salem Street, where the front door of the restaurant was located. It was still early enough that the tourists hadn't descended on the neighborhood, and the only people who were out were residents, like herself. Lucy waved at the owner of the bakery across the street as he unlocked his front door and propped it open.

Continuing down the street, Lucy arrived at the little corner store tucked between two more restaurants at the intersection where Salem Street ended. She headed inside, picking up several copies of the day's paper. "Hi, Rafael," she greeted the man behind the counter. Like most establishments in the neighborhood, the store had been owned by the same person for much of Lucy's life. Rafael smiled and rang Lucy up, offering her a bag. She declined, tucking the papers under her arm and heading back out into the bright morning sunlight.

Once outside, Lucy paused for a moment, admiring the view down Charter Street towards the water. When the road was empty, like it was now, you could see all the way to the end and out over Boston Harbor.

Turning around, Lucy headed around the corner and back down Salem Street to her apartment. She climbed the stairs, checking the time on her watch. *It's almost late enough to call Dad,* she thought to herself. Entering the apartment, she dropped the papers on the coffee table and took off her shoes and coat. *Oh well. I guess I just have to have another cup of coffee.*

Setting the machine to brew, Lucy quickly set up the clothesline and hung the finished load of laundry to dry. Hearing the coffee machine *beep,* indicating it was done brewing, she ducked under the line and poured herself a cup. Finished with the laundry, she settled on the couch with her coffee, flipping through a magazine to kill time until she could call her father.

Finishing her drink, Lucy checked the time, happy to see that it was finally after eight in the morning on the west coast. She grabbed her cell phone and dialed her parents' house, tapping her foot impatiently on the rug while it rang.

"Lucy! Hello, dear," Rita Moretti's warm voice filled Lucy's ear. "This is a surprise," she continued, sounding happy.

"Hi, Mom," Lucy replied. "I'm sorry to call so early. How is everything out there in Washington?" she asked absentmindedly.

"Oh, we're doing just fine out here. The weather is finally starting to warm up. How about you, honey? Is everything okay?" Rita asked, a concerned note in her voice.

"Everything is fine, for the most part. Dad is back today from his fishing trip, right?" Lucy asked hopefully. "I need to ask him some questions. There's been a...debate about who owns the restaurant." Lucy paused. *How do I explain this?* she wondered.

"Lucas Ricci, next door, thinks that his family still owns it, because he doesn't have any proof that Nonno ever bought it. He thinks that Nonno scammed his grandmother and just...stole the restaurant! And even worse, he accused Nonno of murdering Marco Ricci to get him out of the way," Lucy finally said, the words spilling out in a rush.

"Oh honey," Rita said patiently. "Your dad doesn't get back until tomorrow morning," she said regretfully. "But I'll have him call you as soon as he does," Lucy's mother promised her. "I do know, however, that your nonno was a good man, and he would never have pulled something like that, let alone commit the murder that made it possible." Rita paused to take a breath.

"Your grandfather was always talking about what it was like right before the war. People would come into our neighborhood and vandalize cars, and people's homes. Everybody always assumed that Marco was killed by some anti-Italian patriot," she added.

"Besides," Rita continued, "that Lucas was always causing trouble. His parents, they spoiled him. He thinks the world owes him everything on a silver platter," she commented. "Have you tried going down to City Hall and seeing if they have any information on the building?" she asked thoughtfully.

"Actually, that hadn't occurred to me," Lucy admitted. "That's a great idea, Mom. I can't believe I didn't think of it - I've been so worried about this," she told her mother. "I'll go down there today. And I'll try to do some research too, on the things that happened in our neighborhood back then. Maybe I can find out what really happened to Marco," she said, feeling hopeful for the first time since her conversation with Lucas.

"Good. And I'll have your Dad give you a call as soon as he gets in tomorrow," Rita promised. "I know you'll take care of this, sweetheart," she said reassuringly. "You can handle it."

"Thanks, Mom," Lucy replied. "You always know what to do," she continued gratefully, feeling her spirits lift.

"That's what moms are for, sweetheart," Rita replied. "Good luck at City Hall—I hope by the time we talk tomorrow this is all taken care of. Love you, honey."

"Love you too, Mom," Lucy replied. "Talk to you tomorrow."

Lucy hung up the phone and slipped it back into her pocket. Luckily, Boston was a small city, and her restaurant was only a short walk from City Hall. Since there was plenty of time left before Alba opened, she grabbed her jacket and slid on a pair of comfortable shoes before running back out the door.

Lucy walked down Salem Street, towards the heart of the city and away from the peaceful waterfront she had been admiring earlier in the day. She moved past some of the most famous restaurants in the city, marveling at how they already had a line for lunch service, even though it was hardly noon. The sun was high in the sky, burning off the morning chill she had felt earlier in the day.

Lucy smiled at the tourists who loved coming to the North End, walking the cobblestone streets and seeing all the historical landmarks that residents took for granted. Among its brick buildings and narrow lanes, the neighborhood held famous burial sites, historical homes and the Old North Church, which had held the lanterns for Paul Revere's famous midnight ride. Plus, there was delicious food anywhere you looked, with restaurants and bakeries on every block.

As she reached the western edge of the neighborhood, the buildings changed abruptly. The North End was a historical neighborhood, but it was sandwiched between the peaceful harbor and downtown Boston. The divider between Lucy's neighborhood and the rest of the city was a narrow park called the Kennedy Greenway, named after the illustrious family. The park was made up of several different sections, encircling nearly the entire city. It was almost impossibly green this time of year, with the gardens and trees just beginning to bloom, making for a beautiful sight. Some called it the Emerald Necklace, and Lucy loved having it so nearby. It was nice to know there was an oasis in the city just around the corner.

Lucy crossed the Greenway, dodging tourists who were too busy taking photographs to look where they were going. Finally, as she walked past the farmers market where Ally often shopped, she spotted City Hall looming ahead of her. It was made almost entirely of concrete and had been built according to the Brutalist school of architecture—it looked more like a prison than anything else. Lucy had often heard it called the ugliest building in the city, and sometimes the entire state. Lucy always hated having to go inside. The building was somehow always cold and damp, no matter what the weather was like outside.

*Oh well,* Lucy thought to herself as she approached the doors, crossing the plaza outside. *If the answer is in there, I'll find it.*

She took a deep breath and stepped through the sliding glass doors, nodding to the security guard inside. Turning the corner, Lucy headed deeper into the building, following the signs to the city clerk's office.

Finally, she arrived in a small room with a desk at one end, breathless from the long flight of stairs. A young woman with brown hair cropped into a pixie cut was seated at the desk, in a light pink blouse. Her name tag read Clara.

"Welcome to the City Clerk's office," Clara greeted her, smiling. "How may I help you?"

"Hi," Lucy replied, still out of breath. "I'm looking for a bill of sale from around 1941," she told Clara. "Is that something you would have here?" she asked hopefully.

"I can certainly look," Clara replied confidently. "We have all sorts of records here, but things do get less and less organized the further back you go," she warned. "What is the address of the building?"

"Well, shortly before it was sold, a wall was built dividing the building into two. Both have a restaurant on the first floor and living space above. The original address was 210 Salem Street, and after the dividing wall was built, 211 Salem Street was added," Lucy informed her.

"Sure thing," Clara replied, jotting down the address on a slip of paper. "Give me a few minutes to go look—those records haven't been digitized, so I'll have to check the actual files. Feel free to grab a seat," she continued, gesturing at a row of seats on the other side of the waiting room.

Lucy wandered over to the chairs and sank into the one closest to the desk. She could just see the top of Clara's head through a small window behind the desk as she moved through rows and rows of shelves and filing cabinets. Eventually, her head disappeared altogether as she went deeper into the room.

Lucy waited, casually reading the various displays full of facts about Boston on the walls. "Did You Know?" asked one brightly-colored poster. "Boston is home to America's first subway, built in 1897" it continued in a jaunty font.

*Thanks, City Hall,* Lucy thought to herself.

Clara popped back out into the waiting area, carrying a few files. She laid them out on her desk and gestured for Lucy to come over. "Come take a look," she called out.

"So, I don't actually have anything at all on 211 Salem Street," she began. "But I do have a few things for 210. There's some paperwork regarding a renovation going on right now—is that any help to you?" Seeing Lucy shake her head, Clara closed that file and put it on the chair behind her.

"Okay, in that case," she continued, moving to the next folder in her stack, "I have a bill of sale from January of 1938, when a man named Marco Ricci bought the entire building, and then a blueprint from July of that year, when it looks like work was done to divide the basement, commercial space and residential space into two separate units. That's when the second building number was requested."

"And this is everything you have on those two buildings?" Lucy asked, feeling her heart sink. "There's no additional bill of sale, maybe from 1941?"

"Nope. A lot of these records tend to go missing over the years, or never existed in the first place," Clara replied. "I'm sorry not to have been more helpful," she apologized, seeing the disappointed look on Lucy's face.

"No, no, not at all," Lucy said, waving her hand and forcing a smile. "It's not your fault. Thank you for looking."

"My pleasure," Clara replied cheerfully. "Have a wonderful day," she said,sinking back into her chair.

With that, Lucy exited the office empty-handed, heading back down the long flight of stairs and out into the sunlight.

# Chapter 6

"Really?" Ally asked that evening. "Nothing at all, no records of anything?" she continued, shutting the door of the office she and Lucy shared.

"Nothing. She didn't even have a file for our half of the building, only for 210 - Bella Luna. The only mention of us at all is when Marco Ricci requested the second building number for our half," Lucy informed her friend, updating her on the visit to City Hall.

"Damn. So what are you going to do now?" Ally asked, searching through her recipe book while she spoke.

"I tried calling my dad, but he doesn't get back until tomorrow. But, honestly, I don't have a clue. If there's no proof, I certainly can't afford to pay Lucas. We would lose the restaurant," Lucy said, shaking her head.

"Oh man, Luce. Do you think, maybe, you could try talking to Lucas? He must know you don't have that kind of money floating around," Ally said.

"I mean, I can definitely try, but he and I don't really get along," Lucy began. "I'm sure that's part of why he wants the restaurant too. We can certainly act civil, normally, but it goes back to when we were kids. He's never liked me, or our family," Lucy admitted. "I'll try, though. Maybe I'll go next door tonight and see if he's there. They only have half the dining room open because of the renovations, so I'm sure he's not too busy."

"I think that's a really good idea," Ally said encouragingly. "I bet if you just explain things to him, have a civil conversation, he'll back right off." She reached out and laid a hand on Lucy's shoulder as she got up to leave the office. "Everything will be alright, you'll see."

Lucy leaned back in her chair as Ally left the small room, closing the door behind her. The office was suddenly silent, all the noises of the bustling kitchen shut out. She brushed back her hair, using both hands to scrape it up into a ponytail.

*Well, time to get out front,* she thought to herself, checking the clock. After six—the dining room would be filling up as the dinner rush got started.

Stepping out of the office, Lucy was immediately overwhelmed by the heat and noise of the kitchen. A *whoosh* of fire went up from a pan on the range as the cook in front of it added wine to the pan, and laughter rang out from the corner as two dishwashers watched a third one dance. "Coming through, boss!" someone shouted out as they brushed past her.

Lucy paused for a second, taking in all the activity. As much fun as they had, this was a group of people who were working hard to keep her family legacy operating, and who were all depending on her to keep things together.

*If Lucas were to take over, who knows what he would do with it? Would he keep any of these people on as employees?* Lucy wondered to herself. Her reverie was broken as another employee came past the office door. "'Scuse me, boss!" he cried out.

"Alright, alright, I'll get out of the way!" Lucy exclaimed jokingly, tossing her hands up in the air. She smiled. Spending time in the kitchen always managed to lift her mood. There was always a happy feeling there, even when the restaurant was at its busiest.

Lucy headed out to the dining room, steeling herself and putting on a smile. *Time to shake some hands,* she thought. Time spent in the dining room was her most and least favorite part of the job: On one hand, it meant a chance to speak to some of her favorite customers, who had been coming to the restaurant for years. On the other hand, there was always someone with a complaint, no matter how ridiculous.

"Oh Lucy, thank goodness." One of the servers, Amanda, grabbed Lucy as soon as she came through the swinging door into the dining room.

"What's up, Amanda?" Lucy asked, following her into the wait station.

"I have a customer over by the window. He says the air coming through the window is too cold, but he won't let me close it. Can you talk to him?" Amanda requested, looking flustered. She fanned a hand in front of her face. "I did talk to him, but all he did was yell at me," she added.

"Of course," Lucy told her. "Just to be clear, he wants us to change the temperature of the air outside?" she asked the young woman.

"Cor-rect," Amanda confirmed, smiling as she pulled her order pad out of her neatly-tied black apron. "He's over at table twelve, right in front of the window," she continued, gesturing with her head.

"Alright, wish me luck!" Lucy joked as she left the server station and headed across the dining room. Weaving through the tables, she spied the man Amanda must have been talking about. He was sitting at a table of four, waving his hands around as he spoke and gesturing at the window.

"Hello, everybody," she greeted the group as she arrived at the table. "Pardon my interruption. My name is Lucy. How is everything tonight?" she asked the group. One of the women at the table opened her mouth to speak, but was quickly cut off by the older man who had been gesturing. His round red face was topped with wispy white hair, waving gently in the breeze from the open window behind the table.

"Unacceptable, that's how it is!" he exclaimed, his voice nearly cracking. "The temperature of this restaurant is unacceptable. And that girl over there absolutely refused to do anything about it," he said, practically spitting the words out as he gestured at Amanda across the room. "The air coming through this window is absolutely frigid. My wife is freezing," he continued, gesturing at the woman who had tried to speak. She looked very comfortable, in a beautiful emerald-green top that set off her blue eyes and platinum hair.

"I'm so sorry about that, sir. Would you like me to shut the window?" Lucy offered, trying to keep the grin that threatened to spread across her face contained.

"Of course not. You don't offer outdoor dining, so this is the best we can do," the man replied, his voice still angry.

"It is still April, sir. Our outdoor seating will open once the weather is a little warmer," Lucy replied congenially, letting a polite smile sneak through onto her lips.

"Well, frankly I find that totally unacceptable! What are you going to do about this?" the man demanded, pounding his fist on the cloth-covered table.

"Ma'am, would you like me to turn up the heat in the dining room?" Lucy offered, directing her question to the woman.

"Actually, I'm fine," the woman replied, smiling at Lucy. "Don't mind my husband. He thinks I'm more sensitive than I am," she continued, patting his hand where it sat on the table. "You don't have to adjust anything on my behalf. And thank you for coming to check on us. Everything has been wonderful so far," she added.

"Are you the manager here, dear?" the woman asked, her hand still resting on her husband's.

"I am," Lucy replied, "and the owner as well. Alba has been in my family for three generations now," she told the couple.

"Fascinating. You are doing a wonderful job, Lucy," the woman said with a smile. "I'm Andrea, and this is Philip," she said, introducing her husband. She continued to ignore the other couple at the table.

"It's such a pleasure to meet you," Lucy said, her polite smile turning genuine. "I'm so glad to hear you're enjoying everything. Please let me know if I can get you anything else," Lucy told her before turning to walk away, crossing the dining room and heading back to the wait stand, where the servers were watching her.

"Just like that?" Amanda said indignantly. "You just went over and said hello and he was happy?" she exclaimed.

"No, no, he was still plenty upset. His wife just put him in his place," Lucy said with a smile. "And stop staring at him," she added firmly. "He's not stupid, just rude."

Lucy remained at the wait station for a moment, watching the servers move around the dining room. There were plenty of customers waiting to sit down, spilling out onto the sidewalk outside. Lucy walked down the length of the bar to the front of the restaurant.

"Hey, Alex," she said, greeting the host. "How's it going? Long line tonight," she commented, taking in the number of customers still waiting.

"Hey, Lucy. Really busy tonight," he replied, shuffling together a few menus. "We're full right now, and we should do another turn, some tables twice more," he informed her, referring to the amount of times each table would be used that night. Two turns was a good night, and three turns would be a great night.

"Excellent—that's what I like to hear!" she said with a grin. "Do you need anything?" she asked.

"Would you mind grabbing the menus back at the wait station? I'm almost out," Alex requested, turning to greet the next customer in line.

"You got it," Lucy replied, stepping away from the host stand. She completed the errand, noticing as she dropped off the menus that Chris, one of the cooks, was standing inside the dining room, trying to catch her attention.

"I'm heading back into the kitchen," she informed Alex as she left the host stand. "Looks like Chris needs me. Shout if you need anything," she added.

"Sure thing. Thanks," Alex called after her as she headed back to meet Chris.

"What's up?" she asked him, arriving at the back of the dining room.

"Well, uh, the owner from Bella Luna is here. He wants to talk to you. Chef sent me to find you," Chris said nervously, his fingers twining together.

"Oh. Did he say what he wants?" Lucy asked, hoping that maybe Lucas just needed to borrow something. The restaurants on their block were always willing to share, knowing that the next day they might be the ones in need.

"No, but he looks angry," Chris informed her, grimacing sympathetically.

"Oh, great. Thanks for letting me know," Lucy said as she squared her shoulders and headed back through the swinging door into the kitchen. She saw—and heard—Lucas immediately, across the kitchen by the back door. Ally was standing with him, clearly trying to placate him. Lucy hurried across the kitchen.

"This is ridiculous!" Lucas exclaimed, seeing Lucy approaching. "Unacceptable! I demand that you do something about this!" he shouted.

*Geez, how many times am I going to get yelled at today?* Lucy wondered to herself.

"Lucas, I need you to calm down. What are you upset about?" she asked, hoping that none of the cooks were overhearing their conversation.

"Here I am, trying to do you a favor by dropping off these blueprints, and your cooks are verbally abusing me! You should have heard what they were saying!" he cried, his face turning crimson. "It's not at all my fault that your grandfather was a cheat, and a murderer, and this whole operation won't last much longer. I don't deserve to be spoken to like that," he said forcefully. "I know you don't believe in discipline, but you have to do something. No legitimate operation would ever employ people like that," he said, jabbing his finger in the air.

"Lucas, thank you for bringing the documents over. But I will not allow you to stand in my kitchen and verbally abuse me, or my grandfather," Lucy began, trying to keep her temper under control. "As for my employees, they are their own people and I can't control what they say. You should know—I'm sure you hear worse from your own employees in your own kitchen," Lucy retorted, unable to keep her temper in check.

"You can't speak to me that way, either!" Lucas shouted. "And what sort of owner discusses business decisions with her staff? This is none of their business. I demand respect from you and your employees, however much longer your restaurant may be in business. I am *finally* going to get my revenge on your terrible family!" Lucas declared loudly. With that, he held out his arm and dramatically dropped the documents he had been holding to the floor. He watched as they fluttered down, then turned and left through the back door, slamming it behind him.

"What a diva!" Ally exclaimed as the door shut. "What was that? He's a grown man and he just threw a temper tantrum!" she said, bending down to collect the papers. "And revenge? What was that about?" she asked.

"I'm not exactly sure," Lucy said thoughtfully. "Wait a second. That must be what all this is about," she realized. "He's trying to get revenge for a crime he's decided my nonno committed, without any proof," she continued. And he thinks these blueprints will finally allow it to happen," she added, the truth sinking in.

"You need to prove that your nonno is innocent, though," Ally pointed out. "Otherwise, he'll just keep trying, even if you can prove that the restaurant is really yours. He'll just find another way," she added logically.

"I guess," Lucy said dejectedly. "Why was he so upset about the cooks?" she asked Ally. "Who was it? Do you know what they said?" she asked her friend, turning to look at the collection of cooks who were all still staring at them with wide eyes.

"I'm not sure," Ally replied, looking down at the ground. "When I came back to talk to him he was already upset about it."

"How do any of the cooks even know about any of this?" Lucy wondered. "I haven't told anyone except you," she said, looking at her friend.

"Well, I may have, uh, told some of them," Ally admitted. "I'm sorry, I didn't think they would do anything like this. I was just venting," she said, handing the pages she was still holding to Lucy.

"I'm really sorry, Luce," she continued. "I've never seen Lucas like that. He was so angry. Does he do that often?" Ally asked.

"He used to, when we were kids," Lucy replied. "That's why he doesn't like me. I used to poke and prod him until he got all worked up, and then run and hide down in the cellar. He used to get in trouble for being mean to me, when in reality, I was the one who started it every time," she admitted.

"Well, that explains it!" Ally cried.

"I know, I know. But you have to admit, some childhood teasing is no reason to still hate someone thirty years later!" Lucy retorted indignantly. "Plus, apparently he just hates my family," she added sarcastically.

"That's fair. It does seem like an overreaction," Ally replied. "Hey, everybody!" she shouted suddenly, over Lucy's head. "Get back to work!"

With that, the cooks all turned back to their work, and the kitchen was suddenly filled again with noise.

"Listen, Ally, it's getting late. Do you mind if I go upstairs and look these documents over?" Lucy requested, trying to flip through the pages Ally had handed her.

"Of course not. Remember to check on that kitten too," Ally reminded her.

"Oh fine. Are you sure you don't want to take him home?" Lucy asked her friend hopefully.

"Hell no! Now go look at those papers and figure out how to save the restaurant," Ally replied, gently pushing Lucy towards the door. "I'll send someone up with some food for you in a little bit," she continued.

"You always take such good care of me!" Lucy called out as she exited through the back door.

Back up in the apartment, Lucy set the kitten free from the bathroom before skimming the blueprint Lucas had brought, along with the rent receipts. "Well, he's right," she remarked to the kitten, who was carefully inspecting the papers. "Nonno only paid rent through September of 1941. After that, nothing," she said dejectedly. The kitten purred reassuringly.

"I won't find anything new in these," she told the kitten. Thinking for a second, she continued, "Let me see if I can find out anything about the vandalism and attacks in the neighborhood before World War II. Maybe I can at least make some progress towards clearing Nonno of Lucas's accusations of murder," she told him hopefully. The kitten stared back for a moment before starting to chew on the corner of the blueprint Lucas had delivered.

"No, no, no!" Lucy scolded, gently extricating the document from the kitten's tiny teeth. She gathered up all the papers and put them on the kitchen counter, out of reach. On her way back to the couch, she grabbed her ancient laptop. While she waited for it to boot up, she tried to play with the kitten, but he seemed to just want to lounge on his back and stare at the ceiling.

"Okay kitten, have it your way," Lucy muttered as she logged in. Opening up the search engine, she got to work, looking for any evidence of the attacks her mother claimed had happened.

A short while later, she was interrupted by a knock at the door. Lucy jumped up and opened the door, revealing Chris standing on the other side.

"Ally wanted to make sure you ate," he explained, handing over a bowl. "Linguine with vodka sauce. Your favorite," he added with a smile.

"Thanks, Chris," Lucy said gratefully. "And please tell Ally thanks, as well."

"You got it, boss," he said, heading back down the steps. Lucy returned to the couch and sat down, eating as she continued her research.

"Well, kitty," Lucy said, reading from an old Boston Globe article she had found, "it looks like one Jacob Eldridge was arrested in 1941 for murdering an Italian woman, just a few blocks from here." Lucy paused for a second, mulling over the information she had just read.

"I wonder how she died?" she asked the kitten. Continuing to read, Lucy was stunned to discover that the poor woman had been shot in the back, right on the sidewalk. "Exactly the same as Marco Ricci," she breathed. Jacob Eldridge had served a few years in jail for manslaughter, before being released and dying peacefully at home many years later.

The article she was reading reported that the police had been "unable to find a motive for the crime, but that the suspect was being questioned in relation to other crimes in the neighborhood."

"Shameful," Lucy muttered. *That man murdered at least one woman, and maybe more, in cold blood, because of a country she didn't even live in any longer. He should have died in jail,* she thought forcefully.

Reading the line again, Lucy wondered about the "other crimes" mentioned. Opening up a new search, she typed in Jacob Eldridge's name. Scrolling, she found another article, one from after his conviction. "Let's see what this one say, kitty cat," she told the kitten, who was now firmly planted in her lap.

"Eldridge was also under investigation for the murder of a man on Salem Street, committed in a similar fashion, but as of yet, the police have been unable to find any evidence linking him to that crime," she read from the page, hope growing in her chest. She squeezed the kitten close.

"That must have been what happened." she exclaimed. "Jacob Eldridge murdered Marco, as well, but they couldn't find any evidence," she told the kitten. "This Jacob Eldridge guy shot Marco Ricci, because he was on some disgusting anti-Italian rampage. And Nonno always said that Elena Ricci refused to speak of it ever again, after Marco died. I bet Lucas asked her about it, she refused to discuss it, and so Lucas concocted this crazy theory," she realized.

She leaned back against the couch. "So it wasn't Nonno," she said to the kitten, a satisfied tone sneaking into her voice. "Now I just have to figure out how to keep Lucas from taking our restaurant, and all will be right."

Lucy carefully picked up the kitten, depositing him on the couch next to her. He glared up at her indignantly as she stood up and stretched. "I think that's enough research for tonight," she told the little kitten, who jumped up and began to weave around her ankles. "Time for me to go to bed, and you to go back in the bathroom," she told him apologetically.

# Chapter 7

"Well, kitty cat, I guess maybe I should go buy you some real food," Lucy said the next morning, staring at the kitten still occupying her bathroom. He was sitting on the edge of the tub, staring back. "I can't afford to keep feeding you salmon," she continued.

The kitten responded by jumping down and coming over to rub on her legs. "Oh fine!" Lucy said. "I'll get you a real litter box too. No more newspapers for you. Whoever ends up taking you can have that, too," she said, bending down to pet the animal.

He responded with a purr, winding around her legs, back and forth. Lucy stroked down the length of his brown-and-black body, smiling to herself when she reached the end of his white-tipped tail. His fur was looking much healthier and shinier, and his eyes seemed brighter too. She straightened up, reaching her arms out and stretching.

"Alright, kitty, I'll go right now. There's still plenty of time before the restaurant opens." With that, she cracked open the bathroom door and slipped out, using her foot to keep the kitten in the bathroom. "Stay!" she commanded, smiling at his antics. "Just stay right there!"

Free from the kitten, she slipped on her shoes and headed down the stairs. There was a pet store about a mile away from the restaurant, an easy walk on a nice day like today.

Lucy set off, coming to the end of the alley and turning right onto Salem Street, towards downtown and City Hall, the same route she had taken yesterday. As she made her way through the city, she let her mind wander, thinking over Lucas's threats. *I'm glad to have solved at least part of the puzzle, and cleared Nonno's name. Now I just have to work on the rest of it,* Lucy thought to herself.

Distracted by her own thoughts as she walked, her mind wandered to Ally's recent nomination. *It's such an honor for her. It would be nice if there was some sort of award for running restaurants too, not just cooking in them,* she thought, with just a tinge of her earlier jealousy. After college, Ally had the option to go elsewhere, and to see the world—Lucy's only opportunity had been back to Boston, and Alba.

"Oh! Excuse me!" Lucy said she abruptly walked into the back of the person in front of her. "I'm so sorry!" she apologized as the person turned towards her.

"Not at all," replied a familiar voice. "It was my fault."

"Charlie!" Lucy cried. "What are you doing here?" she asked in shock.

"Running errands," replied the tall police officer who had saved her life a few weeks ago when she nearly drowned in the harbor. "I'm off duty until later tonight," Charlie explained, using his free hand to push his light brown hair back. His other hand was loaded down with full shopping bags.

"Of course, of course," Lucy replied nervously. "Same here. I'm actually going to a pet store—I have a cat now. Well, he's not mine, but I have him for now..." She trailed off. "Well, you don't care about that. It was nice to see you again," she said, pulling her jacket closer and preparing to set off.

"Hey, Lucy, wait a second," Charlie said, reaching out and touching her arm, his green eyes flashing apologetically. "I'm sorry I never called. It just didn't seem like you had a great time at dinner."

"Oh no, I did! I thought you were the one who wasn't having fun," Lucy replied, smiling. "I was just nervous. It's been a long time since I was on a date."

"I was nervous too. I haven't had a first date in a long time," Charlie said. "In fact, I had just gotten out of a really serious relationship," he admitted. "I just wasn't sure how to act."

"I understand. I'm sure it's hard," Lucy replied, trying to move away again.

"No, no, I'm doing this all wrong," Charlie said. "I had a great time. I'd like to take you out again," he continued, his hand still resting on her arm.

"Oh," Lucy replied, taken aback. "Sure. I think that would be fun," she agreed hesitantly. "One thing, though," she said, smiling as an idea popped into her head.

"Of course—do you want to pick the restaurant this time?" Charlie asked, returning her smile. "You are the expert."

"Nope—let's make dinner. Together, at my place," she replied. "Trust me, I have any ingredient you could dream of."

"Let's do it! On Monday?" Charlie asked, his smile growing even wider.

"Yes. Say seven o'clock?" Lucy said. "I'll have everything ready—don't worry about bringing anything."

"Sounds like a plan," Charlie said. "I'll see you then," he added, squeezing her arm before letting go and disappearing into the crowd.

*Well, well, well,* Lucy thought to herself. *Who would have thought?*

She continued down the sidewalk, smiling to herself as she moved past the Greenway and towards the heart of the city, where the buildings grew taller and more modern. She passed City Hall, where she had been the day before, and finally arrived at her destination—a small pet shop, surrounded by chain stores and restaurants. It was owned by an old friend of her father's, Theo Hardy. Theo and her father had attended high school together, long ago.

Lucy entered the store and smiled at the older man behind the counter, wearing a brown sweater and thick eyeglasses. "Hi, Theo!" she called out brightly.

"What on earth? That's not Lucy Moretti, is it?" he exclaimed, peering over his glasses at her. "It is!" he cried out, getting up from his stool and coming around the counter. "Lucy, what are you doing here?" he asked as he hugged her.

"Coming to see you, of course!" she answered, returning his hug. "I'll admit, I also need your expertise—I found a kitten behind the restaurant a few days ago," she told him. "I've been feeding it on salmon filets, but I think it's time I get some real cat food."

"Of course, of course, that's what I'm here for," Theo replied, gesturing grandly towards the rest of the store. The aisles, packed full with colorful bags and toys, stretched to the back of the store, to the area where Theo kept his fish—tropical fish were his true passion. The rest of the store was really just a way to support his hobby.

Theo led Lucy to a spot in the middle of the store. "Now, tell me, how is John?" he asked as they walked.

"My dad is doing well," Lucy replied. "He and my mom are enjoying their retirement—they're still living out in Washington. Apparently he's on a fishing trip up in the mountains right now," she continued, feeling overwhelmed by all the cat-themed products she was suddenly surrounded by.

"Good for him!" Theo exclaimed, grinning as he pulled a bag down off of the shelf. "Now, this is what you want. It's kitten food. This'll last the little guy for a few weeks," he explained, showing the bag to Lucy. "Come back once you run out and I'll give you some adult food," he said, handing the bag to Lucy. "I'll let you carry that. My old bones can't handle it!" He laughed. "Now, do you need a litter box? And some toys, of course," he mused, mostly to himself.

He continued collecting items off the shelf, piling them in a small litter box he grabbed from the lower shelf. "Oh, and a nice water bowl too," he muttered, adding it to the increasingly precarious pile.

"Theo, I think that's probably enough," Lucy interrupted, trying to save her arms. The pile was growing taller by the second.

"Nonsense," Theo replied. "You're young and strong!" Finally satisfied with his selection, he topped the pile with one final toy and moved back to the front of the store. He started scanning the items, carefully packing them into a larger cardboard box. "There," he said, pushing the box towards her. "You'll be able to carry that. Now just let me add the discount—"

"Theo, no!" Lucy interrupted again. "I'm happy to pay full price. Don't give me any discount," she insisted.

The old man waved a hand. "Nonsense," he scoffed. "You don't pay full price here!" he cried, waving one hand as the other continued pecking at his register.

"Well, promise me that you'll come by the restaurant sometime and have dinner, my treat," Lucy conceded, handing over her credit card.

"Well, if it'll make you happy," he said with a shrug and smile. "Alright, you're all set." He handed the card back. "Have some fun with that kitten of yours! What's its name?" he asked as Lucy carefully returned the card to her wallet.

"Uh, I haven't really thought about that. I'm not planning on keeping it, I just need to find someone who wants a cat. How about you?" Lucy asked hopefully.

"Oh no, dear," Theo said, shaking his head. "I can't have a cat—they're absolutely terrible around my aquariums. But I'll certainly ask around and see if anyone is looking," Theo offered. "If you want to make a flyer, I'd be happy to put it up in the store," he offered, gesturing to the bulletin board near the door filled with similar notices.

"Well, thank you, Theo," Lucy said. "If I can't find anyone else I'll definitely do that. And thanks for all your help—I would have been lost without you!" She lifted the box, holding back a groan as she did so.

Lucy exited the store and headed home, lugging the heavy box. Nearly half an hour later, she finally arrived back on Salem Street, exhausted. "Damn, Theo," she muttered as she climbed the stairs. "Young and strong, my ass." She pushed open the front door and was immediately greeted by the small *meow* of the little tabby kitten.

"How did you get out?" she cried, struggling to cross the threshold without dropping the box on the kitten now weaving around her legs. She glanced across the room; the bathroom door sat half-open. "What, you know how to open doors now, too?" she asked the kitten, sighing.

She made it across the room and set the large box down on the coffee table, sighing in relief as she straightened up. The kitten jumped up on the table, eagerly sniffing the outside of the box. "You smell something interesting, don't you?" Lucy asked as she stroked his tiny back.

She unpacked the box, finding just about anything a kitten could ask for. Theo had sent her home with food, litter, treats and more toys than any cat could play with. There was even a little bed tucked in the bottom of the box. "Salmon treats," Lucy commented with a wry smile as she laid everything out on the table.

The kitten was meowing frantically, rubbing its face all over the bag of food. "What, you're hungry?" Lucy asked as she pulled out the matching ceramic food and water bowls Theo had included. They were painted light blue, one with a large, smiling water droplet on the inside and the other with an equally sized fish on the inside. Setting them down, she ripped a small hole in the bag and poured out some food into the bowl with the fish, laughing as the kitten eagerly tried to eat from the waterfall of kibble. "Be patient!" Lucy scolded gently. The bowl filled, she watched the kitten eat for a moment before filling the water bowl and putting it down next to the food next to the coffee table.

Lucy moved around the apartment, setting up the bed on the floor in her bedroom and scattering the toys around. She even found a little mat at the bottom of the box, for the food and water bowls to sit on.

*Wow, Theo sure knows how to spoil a cat,* she thought to herself, watching as the tabby kitten zigzagged around the room, playing with one toy and then another.

"Oh shoot," Lucy said out loud to the little kitten. "Dad is back today. I should try calling." She checked the clock on the wall—it was nearly one in the afternoon. "Perfect timing," she commented out loud. "Plenty of time before the restaurant opens."

## Chapter 8

Lucy sat down on the couch and slipped her cell phone out of her pocket. The kitten bounded over and climbed up on her lap, rubbing against her chin. "Kitty cat, calm down," Lucy scolded gently. "I have to make a call."

She dialed the number to her parents' house, holding her breath. The phone rang, seemingly forever, before her father's deep voice filled her ear.

"Lucy! My dear, how are you?" he asked. Lucy could practically hear the smile in his voice.

"Hi, Dad. I'm doing well. How was your fishing trip?" she asked.

"Didn't catch a damn thing, except a cold," John replied, sniffling. "It was worth it, though. One of these days I'm gonna have to get you out here so you can see what real mountains are like."

"One of these days, Dad." Lucy said absentmindedly. "Listen, I have to talk to you about something," Lucy said, feeling her nervousness rise up inside her. "I need to tell you something."

"I know, Lucy," he responded quickly, his tone soothing. "Your mom told me. Why don't you fill in the details for me, though? Why, exactly, does Lucas think he still owns our restaurant? And why the heck is he accusing my father of killing someone?" her father asked.

"Okay," Lucy started, taking a deep breath. "First things first, I don't think Nonno murdered anyone. I found a news article from 1941 about a guy, Jacob Eldridge, who was committing hate crimes against Italians in the North End," she told her father. "He actually killed a woman, just a few blocks from here, by shooting her in the back outside her home, and was under suspicion for doing the same thing to another person, who wasn't named in the articles I found. I think it was Marco Ricci," Lucy said, pausing for a breath.

"But there wasn't any evidence, and so Eldridge only went to jail for killing that poor woman. But didn't Nonno always say that Elena refused to talk about it, ever again?" she asked. Not waiting for an answer, she rushed on with her theory. "But if Eldridge was never actually arrested for the crime, and Elena refused to ever speak of it again, then Lucas would have come up with his own conclusion, which is apparently that Nonno did it," she added.

"That certainly makes more sense than my dad doing it," her father said, finally getting a chance to speak. "What a horrible, horrible thing to do to a family," he said sadly.

"I know," Lucy said sadly. "As for the building, that's still a question mark. Here's what I know so far," she said, launching into her next monologue.

"I was able to find out that Marco Ricci purchased and divided the building in 1938. And then in 1939, Nonno opened Alba, but was paying rent to Marco Ricci. In 1941, right after Marco died, the rent payments stopped. Or at least, the only records of rent payments that Lucas has, end in 1941," Lucy replied, trying to speak as clearly as she could. "And now, Lucas thinks that he owns our half of the restaurant, and he wants us to either pay him back rent for the last sixty-odd years, or buy the building. He says he'll evict us if we can't pay. He thinks that Nonno somehow scammed his grandmother," she finished, out of breath.

"Well, this all happened long before I was born," John said thoughtfully. "But I know for a fact that my father was a good man. He would never have done something like that, especially not to a grieving widow," he added.

"That's exactly what I said!" Lucy interrupted. "But how do we prove it?" she asked.

"That's what I was getting to—my father always used to say something to me. Occasionally, he would talk about getting older, and he would always say that, when the time was right, he had something to show me in the cellar. But, of course, he died much sooner than anyone was anticipating," Lucy's father replied.

"Well, his diet of entirely pasta certainly didn't help," Lucy said with a wry laugh. "But what's this about the cellar? Do you have any idea what he might have been talking about?" she asked.

"Not a clue," her father replied, his voice regretful. "I never got to ask him. But you and I both know how unorganized his file keeping could be—and how much he liked to stash things away in unusual places. I think you should take a peek down there, see if there could be anything important," he continued.

"I agree. Thank you, Dad. This feels like it could be the answer," Lucy said, smiling as she absentmindedly petted the kitten that was still sitting on her lap.

"I think so too. Let me know what you find. If you come up empty, I can always try giving Lucas a call myself. Or I can call his father," John offered.

"No, Dad, I don't need you to fight my battles," Lucy said firmly. "But thank you. I'll let you know after I look. Thank you for the help," she continued.

"Of course, honey. Your mother says hello. I'll talk to you soon," her father responded before hanging up the phone.

"Alright, little kitty. Looks like we have some hunting to do," Lucy said. "But you can't help. Let me call up Ally." With that, she dialed the phone again, quickly explaining everything to her friend.

"Can you meet me in the cellar?" Lucy asked.

"Luce, I'm already here!" Ally replied with a laugh. "I was in the kitchen anyway, working on a new sauce. Come on down."

"On my way!" Lucy replied, pushing the kitten off of her lap before hanging up the phone. She stood up and went straight out the door, not bothering to lock the kitten up again. Clearly he could work the doors anyway.

She rushed down the stairs and through the back door of the restaurant, passing the stainless steel dish machine and the spotless prep tables. The door to the cellar stairs was just past her office door, in the long hallway that ran along the back wall of the kitchen. Lucy reached the door and pushed it open, watching it swing out into the open space over the staircase. She reached for the light switch, but, of course, Ally had already flipped it.

"Hey, Ally!" she called out as she descended the stairs. The cellar was larger than it seemed at first glance, holding the lockers for the employees, a small bathroom and the wine cellar that served the restaurant upstairs.

"Hey, Lucy!" Ally's voice responded. "I'm in the wine cellar. Seemed like the best place to start," she called out, her voice echoing on the stone and brick walls.

Lucy finished descending the stairs and crossed the open space in front of the lockers, her gaze pausing momentarily on a large locker in the middle. It had "Donny" scrawled across it in black marker. It had belonged to Donovan Fagan, a longtime employee of the restaurant, who had been tragically murdered a few months before. The locker was still empty—a gesture of respect from the other employees.

Lucy shook her head to chase away thoughts of Donovan, and entered the wine cellar.

"There you are!" she exclaimed as she caught sight of her friend's golden curls on the other side of the room.

"Here I am!" replied Ally. "I thought it made sense to start in here. Didn't you tell me once that all these wine racks are original?"

"They are," Lucy confirmed, nodding her head. She tucked a piece of hair behind her ear. "My grandfather built them himself when Alba first opened. I agree, this has to be the right spot." Lucy replied, running a hand down the rack closest to her. "Do you want to take the whites, and I'll take the reds?" she offered. The wines were arranged with the white wines on the left-hand side and the red wines on the right-hand side. The most popular bottles of wine were closest to the door, with the least popular, and most expensive, at the back.

"Heard," Ally replied, using a kitchen term as she moved to the left side. The two women got to work, chatter fading into silence as they focused.

They went over every single rack from top to bottom, even crawling on the floor to check the undersides. An hour later, they were forced to admit defeat.

Lucy finally spoke. "Okay, well, I don't think there's anything in here. We've gone over every inch of the racks, and there's no other place in the wine cellar to hide anything," she admitted.

"I agree," Ally said with a sigh. "What else was here when your grandfather was in charge?" she asked, leaning against the rack. There was a sudden smash as a bottle crashed to the floor, and Ally jumped back.

"Oh shoot, Lucy, I'm sorry!" Ally apologized as both women watched the red wine running across the flagstone floor. "I'll go get some rags and a trash bag—be right back!" she cried out as she took a large step over the spilled wine and jogged across the cellar. The room was quickly filled with the bright, fruity smell of the wine.

"It's fine—get the broom too!" Lucy called after her. While she waited for Ally to return, she carefully turned over the shards until she found the one she was looking for. The label revealed that the bottle was the house red wine, nothing expensive.

*Phew,* Lucy thought to herself. They didn't carry any truly absurdly priced wine, but there were still a few bottles that would hurt to lose.

Ally came back down, arms loaded with supplies. "Here, let me clean up the puddle of wine," she said, carefully kneeling down.

"I'll start getting the big pieces," Lucy offered, grabbing the garbage bag. In a few moments, it was as if nothing had ever happened. Ally grabbed the garbage bag and hurried upstairs, depositing it in the trash before heading back down.

"You know, an award-winning chef would never drop a bottle of wine," Lucy said as she arrived, trying to joke.

"And if they gave awards to restaurant owners, you would never win with such wobbly wine racks," Ally retorted. Both women eyed each other for a moment before breaking into cautious smiles.

"Alright, now where were we?" Ally asked.

"Trying to figure out where else to look," Lucy replied. "Not the lockers—those weren't installed until after my grandfather died. I don't know about the bathroom. That could be original, I suppose," Lucy continued, shrugging.

"Let's go take a look," Ally suggested, checking her watch. "But it is almost three. We have to get upstairs soon," she added.

"The bathroom isn't very big—let's take a quick look. Maybe behind the toilet or the mirror?" Lucy wondered as they crossed the cellar to the tiny bathroom, tucked underneath the stairs. Lucy pulled open the door, stepping inside.

Lucy carefully examined the mirror and the sink, looking for anything that seemed out of place. There was nothing; it was just an only vanity. She turned around, crouching down to check behind the toilet. Carefully, Lucy lifted up the lid on the back of the toilet, covering the tank. "You always see people hide things in here on TV," she explained to her friend. "But unfortunately, it looks like Nonno didn't think of that," she added in a dejected tone after finding nothing.

"We really need to make sure that the toilet gets cleaned more often," Ally commented, wrinkling her nose. "One of us should really come down here and inspect everything once a week," she added.

"I'll let you have that honor," Lucy said, replacing the lid to the toilet tank. "I don't see anything," she added. "Is there anywhere else you can think of to check in here?" she asked, glancing around the tiny room.

"Nope," Ally replied in a disappointed tone. "The floor seems normal, right?"

"Completely," Lucy replied with a sigh. "I was really hoping it would be in there. I don't know where else to look," she admitted, exiting the tiny room and closing the door.

"Could it have been in some piece of furniture that's been moved?" Ally wondered.

"I have no idea," Lucy replied dejectedly. "I wish at least one of the people involved in this was still alive. It would be so much easier if I could just call up my Nonno or Nonna, or even Elena," she added with a sigh.

"You really miss them, don't you," Ally said, leaning against the wall.

"I really do," Lucy admitted. "After they retired and my parents took over Alba, my grandparents took care of me every day. Nonno died when I was still pretty young, but my nonna was around for a while, and she'd walk me to school and pick me up every day," she added, a smile on her lips. "Oh well," she said, taking a deep breath. "I was lucky to have as much time with them as I did."

"Anyway," Lucy said, going back to the subject at hand, "As far as I know, there was never anything else down here," Lucy continued, rubbing her hand down the rough brick wall. "My grandfather finished the basement himself—there was no one else who could have taken anything, except for all the employees we've had over the years."

"You really think one of them could have found something, and stolen it?" Ally asked in surprise.

"No, not really," Lucy admitted. "For the most part, they've all been good people, even going back to the beginning. My nonno prided himself on not hiring just anyone, and he taught that to me and my dad. I know if one of them had found something that looked important, they would have given it to us," Lucy added as they both headed up the stairs back to the kitchen.

"We'll look again," Ally promised. "We'll come down tomorrow morning, and all day Monday if we have to. We'll find it, if it's still here."

"Oh! I have to tell you something!" Lucy exclaimed, suddenly remembering her big news. "Guess who I ran into this morning? Literally, I mean."

"Literally? Like, you actually ran into someone?" Ally asked, laughing. "Who on earth did you run into?" she continued.

"Charlie Fitz! The police officer who…" Lucy trailed off as Ally interrupted.

"Who investigated Donovan's murder! And asked you out on a date, and never called afterwards!" Ally exclaimed. "You saw him? Where? What did he have to say for himself?" Ally peppered Lucy with questions as they stepped into the small office and sat down. "Shut the door and tell me everything!" Ally demanded.

"I went to a pet store, to get some stuff for the cat. On the way, I bumped into him. He apologized for never calling, said he was nervous," Lucy told her friend excitedly. "We actually made plans for Monday night. He's going to come over and we'll make dinner together. I thought that seemed a lot more relaxed than going out again," she explained.

"Good idea," Ally said, nodding approvingly. "What are you going to make? Do you need a recipe?" she asked eagerly.

"I was thinking pasta carbonara—what do you think? It's easy, but delicious," Lucy replied. "I can prep everything beforehand and just have to boil the water once he arrives," she added.

"I think the carbonara is a great idea!" Ally exclaimed. "And what about the wine—a nice dry Zinfandel, maybe?" she continued excitedly. "And dessert! You need dessert! I'll whip something up," she declared.

"Ally, stop! You don't need to make us dessert. I can go to the bakery across the street for cannoli," Lucy protested.

"Absolutely not! I'll make a nice little fruit tart, something light after the heavy pasta," Ally continued, cutting her friend off. "And you need a salad to start too. What about a nice, simple, mixed-green salad? With peach slices and walnuts and a raspberry vinaigrette? Don't worry, I'll make that too." She paused for a second. "Do you think you should take up some of the nice plates from the restaurant?"

"Ally, no! My plates are perfectly fine. We're going to have a low-key evening, not a catered meal. But, if you want to make dessert, I will graciously accept your offer of a fruit tart," Lucy conceded, laughing.

"Oh fine! But it'll be the best damn fruit tart you've ever had," Ally retorted, a smile lighting up her pretty face.

"Trust me, I know!" Lucy replied. "But for now, let's get out front. Who knows what the employees have been up to while we've been playing detective?" The two women rose out of their chairs and exited the office, Ally turning left and heading deeper into the kitchen, while Lucy turned right and headed past the cellar door, out into the dining room.

"Hey, Lucy!" a voice called out. It was Alex, one of the restaurant hosts. "Someone left this for you," he said, hurrying over. He handed Lucy a business card. "One of the customers last night. She said you were great and told me it was really important that you get this," he continued.

"Thanks, Alex," Lucy said, looking at the card. "Do you remember who it was?" she asked curiously.

"Yeah, actually, it was the lady who was here with the old guy who was so upset about the window last night," Alex responded. "I don't know what she wanted," he said over his shoulder as he returned to the host stand.

Lucy read the card. "Andrea Anders" was the name printed on it, followed by the words "Lead Consultant—Anders Restaurant Group". *A restaurant group?* Lucy thought to herself. *It must be another offer to buy the building.* Lucy had gotten several offers over the years from people who wanted to buy the building the restaurant was located in. It was prime North End real estate, and big restaurant groups were constantly looking for properties to open new, seemingly-independent restaurants—which inevitably pushed small, actually independent restaurants, like Alba, out of business.

She tucked the card into her pocket and headed over to check on the rest of the front-of-house employees. Some were working hard, preparing for the evening ahead, and some were taking things a little more slowly.

"Come on, folks!" she called out, clapping her hands. "Let's get ready to go—it's almost time to open!"

# Chapter 9

Lucy awoke with a start. She had only been in bed for a short while; she had been stuck downstairs in the restaurant until two in the morning. There had been a couple that lingered over their bottle of wine before leaving hand in hand around midnight.

She blinked in the darkness, trying to remember the dream she had been having. She had been dreaming about her nonno. Slowly, it was coming back to her.

*What a bizarre dream,* she thought to herself. In it, she had been small again, a child. In the dream she had been looking up at her nonno, laughing, because he was being silly. They had been playing a game together, but he kept insisting that it was important, that she needed to listen.

Lucy sat up in bed, replaying the dream over and over again. *Was that real?* she thought. Slowly, a memory began to form in her head, from when she had been very young. She could remember standing on the stairs leading down to the cellar, with Nonno standing over her, insisting that she pay attention.

"Lucy, this is very important!" Lucy could hear his booming voice in her head, with a trace of his Italian accent, even so many years after departing his home country. "Lucy, my girl, you have to pay attention!" the memory continued. Nonno had picked her up and had used his hand to guide hers to a spot on the brick wall along the stairs. She could remember the way his short white beard had brushed against her cheek. "Remember this, Lucy," he had said solemnly. "This is important."

Lucy shook her head, still sitting up in bed. *That can't be real,* she thought. *Can it?* Absentmindedly, she stroked her hand over the head of the kitten sleeping next to her, curled up on her bed, totally ignoring the new cat-sized one she had purchased for him earlier that day. He twitched, as if having a dream of his own.

Lucy rolled out of bed and made her way to the kitchen, filling a glass of water and leaning against the counter as she sipped. The kitten came padding out of the bedroom, letting out a short mew before sitting at her feet.

Lucy stared out the window above her sink, overlooking Salem Street. The bakery across the street had its van parked out front, and two very unhappy-looking teenagers were slowly loading it with freshly baked bread.

*I can almost smell that fresh bread from here,* Lucy thought. All of a sudden, she remembered she had never had dinner the night before. *I wonder if that's the reason for the weird dream,* she thought to herself.

"Just to be safe, better have a snack," she told the kitten, shrugging. She opened the cabinet and pulled out a loaf of the same bread that was being loaded into the truck across the street. Popping a slice into the toaster, she bent down to pet the kitten while she waited. She heard the truck across the street rumble to life and pull away. *Poor kids,* Lucy thought to herself as she straightened up. The toaster popped and Lucy pulled out the bread, spreading butter over it and eating so quickly she burnt her fingers.

"Mmm," Lucy said out loud. "Sorry I can't share, little guy. That was delicious," she told the kitten as she washed her hands. As she dried them, she finally checked the time and was surprised to discover it was almost five in the morning.

"Come on, kitty," she said out loud as she emptied her glass into the sink. "Time to go back to bed."

# Chapter 10

Lucy awoke around eight the next morning, remembering her dream from the middle of the night. *That couldn't have been real, could it?* she wondered.

She slowly climbed out of bed, stretching. The memory she had uncovered stayed at the front of her mind as she showered and made her coffee, until finally, she couldn't take it anymore. She quickly got dressed in a long-sleeved t-shirt and black yoga pants, calling Ally as she did.

"Hey, Ally, I'm sorry to call you so early," she said to her friend. "I had this crazy dream last night, and I have another idea of where to search, down in the cellar. Do you think maybe you could come over?" she asked.

"Yeah, sure," Ally replied, muffling a yawn. "I'll be there in fifteen. Have coffee waiting."

"You got it," Lucy replied with a laugh. "I'll meet you in the cellar," she added.

While she waited for more coffee to brew, Lucy paced impatiently around the apartment, tidying up. It was tough to keep the mess under control in such a small apartment, especially when you spent nearly every waking moment at work like she did. Having the kitten staying with her certainly hadn't helped either.

When the machine beeped, Lucy quickly prepared a mug for her friend—just a splash of milk, the way Ally liked it. Carefully carrying both mugs, her own now half-empty, Lucy made her way down the back stairs and into the restaurant, fumbling to unlock the doors with her hands full. She finally made it over to the cellar steps, where she flicked on the light and sat down to wait for Ally.

Just a moment later, she heard the back door creak open, and Ally's voice calling her name. "Over here!" she called back. Ally came down the steps and sat down on the same tread as Lucy. "Scootch over," she said, bumping Lucy with her hip as she reached over to take her mug of coffee. She took a long sip.

"Okay, now I can talk," she said, before taking another. "What's going on? You had a dream?" she asked.

"Yeah. I know it sounds crazy, but I had a dream about Nonno, and that triggered this memory," Lucy told her friend, both hands wrapped tightly around the warm mug she was holding. "It wasn't a lot, but I remember him telling me, over and over again, that it was important," Lucy replied. "We were standing right here on these stairs, and he picked me up and made me touch the wall. He kept saying how important it was that I remember."

"Well, that's interesting," Ally said thoughtfully. "Do you know which part of the wall?" she asked before taking another sip.

"No, I don't. It was definitely this wall, though. We were standing on the stairs, and I remember all the bricks. This is the only staircase inside the building. Even the staircase outside, to the apartment, has a stucco wall, not brick," Lucy pointed out.

"Well, then, I guess we'd better start looking!" Ally said, heaving herself up. She reached out a hand to pull Lucy up to standing position. "Do you want to start at the top of the stairs, and I'll start at the bottom?" she asked.

"Sure," Lucy replied. "Shout if you see anything weird," she continued, climbing back up to the top of the staircase, while Ally headed down to the bottom.

Lucy started to inspect the wall, feeling a little silly as she did so. "Does this make you feel kind of crazy?" she called down the stairs to Ally.

"Yeah, I mean, I don't think a lot of sane people spend time inspecting brick walls. But hey, we work in a restaurant! We already knew we were crazy," Ally joked.

"Fair enough," Lucy replied, laughing as she went back to her task. "Do you see anything yet?" she asked.

"Nothing yet," Ally replied. "Anything up there?" she asked hopefully.

"Actually, yes," Lucy said slowly. "There's a brick here, with no mortar," she said excitedly, running her fingers over the brick in question. She set her cup of coffee down on the stairs, using both hands to try and move the brick.

"That sounds promising!" Ally called back excitedly. She abandoned her section of the wall and hurried up the stairs to meet Lucy.

"I can't quite get a grip on it," Lucy said, struggling to grasp the very edge of the brick. "Here, help me," she continued, making room for Ally to fit in next to her. Together, they managed to wiggle the brick out of the wall. Behind it, carefully folded to fit the space, was a piece of paper.

"Oh my gosh," Lucy said in disbelief. She reached into the hole left by the brick and was just able to grab the paper with her fingertips.

"What is it?" Ally asked eagerly, peering over Lucy's shoulder.

"Let's find out," Lucy replied, gingerly unfolding the paper. A second, smaller piece of paper fluttered out as she did so.  Ally bent down to pick it up.

"This is...a bill of sale," Lucy said in astonishment, "dated September 19th, 1941. For our half of the building—211 Salem Street. Purchased by Angelo Moretti, from Elena Ricci, for $7,150," she read from the piece of the paper. "Can you believe it? This is it!" she exclaimed, excitement lighting up her face.

"And this is a letter," Ally said, reading from the paper she was holding. "From the same date. It's addressed to Angelo, from Elena, and it thanks him for helping her to keep Bella Luna operating after her husband 'was killed by that evil man'?" she read, quoting the letter. "Killed by that evil man?" she asked Lucy, raising an eyebrow.

"So she knew that Eldridge did it," Lucy said in disbelief. "I was reading about this. There was this guy, Jacob Eldridge, who went to jail for committing hate crimes against Italians before World War II," she explained. "He was only charged with one murder, but I think he may have killed Marco Ricci as well," she added. "This is it!" she exclaimed, clutching the document to her chest. "The proof that my Nonno didn't murder anyone! Elena Ricci certainly wouldn't have sold a building to her husband's murderer, would she?"

"I doubt it," Ally agreed. She continued reading. "She says that she wouldn't have been able to keep Bella Luna open without the money your grandfather paid for Alba."

"Wow," Lucy said in awe. "So not only was he *not* a scheming crook, *or* a murderer, like Lucas wanted him to be, he stepped up and saved the day for the Riccis. I can't believe we found this," she said, her voice rising in excitement as she grasped her friend's arm. "This has to be enough, right? There's no way Lucas can try to fight this!" Lucy exclaimed. "Let's go talk to him right now!"

"Luce, it's only just past eight in the morning," Ally protested." He keeps the same kind of hours we do. He may be a jerk, but we can't go knock on his door this early. Why don't we go upstairs and have another cup of coffee?" Ally suggested, always the voice of reason.

"Oh fine," Lucy sighed. "I can't believe Nonno hid the bill of sale behind a brick—he was crazy!" she exclaimed. "What if I had never remembered that moment, and we lost the building?" she wondered out loud, holding the papers to her chest and sinking down to sit on the stair. Ally sat next to her.

"But you did," Ally pointed out. "He believed in you."

"He was still crazy," Lucy said affectionately. "My crazy old Nonno. I really miss him," she said suddenly. "I wish he was still around today to see what this place has turned into," she continued, rubbing her finger on the brick she still held.

Ally put her arm around Lucy and squeezed. "You've done a good job here, Luce," she said. "Your grandfather would be proud."

They sat together for a moment in silence before Ally spoke again.

"Well, we have had a very exciting morning," she commented. "What do you say about that second cup of coffee, and then we'll go talk to Lucas?"

"Yeah, that's a good idea," Lucy said, clutching the bill of sale and letter closer to her chest. "I want to get these put away safely before anything can happen to them." Standing up, she carefully returned the brick to it's spot in the wall before heading back up to the top of the stairs.

Emerging from the cellar doorway, they were heading towards the back door when Lucy stopped short. "What's wrong?" Ally asked.

"Look," Lucy said, gesturing. "There's someone in the dining room." Looking through the glass window in the swinging door between kitchen and dining room, Lucy could just see the silhouette of someone peering over the bar. They had their back to the swinging door, and Lucy couldn't tell who it was.

"What the hell? Let's go," Ally said, pulling Lucy's arm as they switched direction and headed out to the darkened dining room.

"Excuse me, but we don't open until five o'clock," Lucy said firmly as they moved through the swinging door, Ally leading the way.

"I know. Just checking out what will soon be mine," Lucas announced as he turned around. "You left the back door open. Really poor operational skills. Things like that will never happen once I'm in charge," he continued, moving closer.

"Lucas!" Lucy exclaimed in shock. "This is totally unacceptable. You need to leave, now," she added forcefully. "You have absolutely no right to come into my restaurant uninvited," she continued. "And it is, in fact, my restaurant. I have the proof right here," she said, waving the documents they had discovered in the brick wall. "So get out. Now!" she exclaimed.

"Proof? I don't believe you for a second," Lucas said angrily. "Let me see those. Are those the only copies?" he demanded, reaching a hand out.

"I am most certainly not going to hand these to you, Lucas. I will give them to my lawyer, who will show them to your lawyer," Lucy said, trying to keep her voice steady. "We're going to do this officially. Besides, I don't trust you with these documents for one second!" she exclaimed, taking a step backwards and holding the papers close.

"It's a bill of sale, Lucas," Lucy continued. "Dated mid-September, 1941. Signed by Elena Ricci. And guess what else? A letter, thanking my grandfather for his generosity. By purchasing our building, he gave your grandmother the funds to keep Bella Luna open. So really, I think you owe our family an apology, and a thank-you. Bella Luna wouldn't exist today if it wasn't for Angelo Moretti," Lucy continued confidently.

"And," she said, taking a deep breath, "my nonno certainly did not shoot your grandfather. You should feel ashamed for suggesting such a thing. Some low-life was committing hate crimes in the neighborhood back then, and he was the only who did it. Elena practically says so in this letter," she added, holding up the letter triumphantly.

Lucas's face seemed to contort right before her, twisting into anger. "My grandmother did no such thing!" he cried out. "She never mentioned my grandfather again. You're lying," he added cruelly.

Lucy held up the paper and read. "I am also grateful for your help after Marco was killed by that evil man. I regret that the police were unable to prove it, but at least he will be in prison for quite some time, if for other crimes," she recited, reading Elena's words to Lucas.

"This is your grandmother's handwriting, correct?" she asked confidently, holding the paper up where Lucas could see it.

You really think that solves all your problems?" he snarled, trying to grab it. "Don't worry. Sooner or later you'll run this place into the ground, and I'll be here waiting. I'll take back what my family deserves, *puttana*!" he exclaimed, cursing in Italian. He knocked his shoulder into Lucy's as he strode towards the door back into the kitchen.

"Hey! You need to apologize!" Ally cried out. When Lucas didn't answer, it was followed by an indignant, "Jackass!"

The back door slammed closed, indicating that Lucas had left the restaurant. Lucy took a deep breath, reining in her temper, and led the way back to the kitchen office.

"I hate him," she declared as she sat down. "Why is he so obsessed with my family?" she wondered.

"Maybe he's just jealous, deep down," Ally said as they both sat. "You got to grow up with a grandfather who was alive, and a grandmother who wasn't scarred by loss," she pointed out. "You got to have a happy childhood."

"I did," Lucy said thoughtfully. "I did have a happy childhood, but I spent it teasing him," she realized. "Never about his grandparents, or anything cruel, but I did spend my childhood tormenting him," she added. "Wow. I kind of feel like I owe him an apology," she admitted to Ally, her shoulders drooping as she sank back into her chair.

"That might be a good idea, but I think it's best to just let him be for now," Ally counseled, running a hand through her blonde curls. "Maybe in a few days, if you still feel like it, you can go over and try to clear the air," she suggested. "Besides, maybe he just hates you because Alba is more successful than Bella Luna!" she added with a chuckle.

"That could always be true, too," Lucy admitted with a rueful grin. "You know what, I'll take it," she said, pushing her wavy hair back out of her face. "I need a win right now," she continued with a wry laugh.

"Well, you got one!" Ally replied. "Are you going to call your dad and give him the good news?" she asked.

"Of course, but I'm going to have to wait a little longer. It's barely six in the morning out west," Lucy pointed out to her friend.

"Fair enough," Ally conceded. "Listen, why don't we go upstairs and have that second cup of coffee?” she asked. “I think we’ve earned it at this point.”

# Chapter 11

*I really can't believe it,* Lucy thought to herself as she finally sank down onto her couch later that day. Ally was downstairs in the restaurant getting ready for dinner service, and Lucy had taken the chance to finally sit down and take a breath.

*I can't believe we actually found the papers,* she thought gratefully. *I can't believe Nonno hid them in a brick wall. Crazy old man,* she thought affectionately.

The kitten came out of the bedroom and jumped up on the couch next to her. Lucy stroked his back, saying, "Looks like we get to stay here awhile longer, kitty cat." She paused for a second. "Or at least I do. I'll find you somewhere nice to live, promise," she told the little kitten. He stared up at her before headbutting her hand.

"Oh fine," Lucy said, "I'm sorry I stopped petting you." She continued stroking his head while she used her other hand to pull out her cell phone.

"Finally time to call Mom and Dad and tell them the good news," she told the kitten while she dialed.

The first ring had barely completed before someone picked up the other end. "Lucy?" came her father's voice over the line. "Hold on, let me get your mother too," he continued, without waiting for an answer.

"Okay, Dad," Lucy said into the silence with a smile. There was a fumble at the other end, and then the speakerphone was switched on.

"No, no, John, it's not turned on!" came her mother's voice. "You have to hit the button," Rita continued.

"Hey, guys!" Lucy called out. "I'm here. I can hear both of you!" she continued, muffling her laughter. Her parents were not the most technologically advanced.

"Oh, good, we can hear you too," came her mother's voice again.

"So what's going on, Lucy? Any updates?" her father said in a concerned tone.

"I have good news," Lucy said. "Great news, actually. I found the bill of sale, from September of

1941. Nonno bought the restaurant from Elena Ricci right after her husband was murdered. I actually found a letter too, from Elena, thanking Nonno for his help. I guess his buying Alba was what allowed Bella Luna to stay in business," Lucy explained to her parents. "And even better, she talks about Marco's murderer in the letter, which means that it definitely wasn't Nonno."

"I knew it!" cried her mother. "Good for you, sweetheart!" her father exclaimed at the same time. "I knew you would do it. That Lucas was always up to no good. He's a scoundrel, through and through," Rita added firmly, a note of anger in her sweet voice.

"To be fair, he did think it was the truth," Lucy conceded. "But he didn't have to be such an ass about it."

"Lucy, watch your mouth," her mother said absentmindedly. Lucy exchanged an amused look with the kitten.

"But wait," John interrupted. "Where did you find it? It's not like he left any files behind. Trust me, I searched that place high and low when he died," he continued.

"Are you ready for this?" Lucy asked. "You'll never guess. The bill of sale, and the letter, were hidden behind a brick in the wall along the cellar stairs!" She told them triumphantly.

"Lucy, what on earth?" her mother cried out.

"How did you know to look there?" her father asked, their voices overlapping again.

"I had this crazy dream. I'm still not sure if it was about something that really happened or not. But in it, Nonno took me down to the cellar, and he made it into a game. He kept making me touch this one specific brick on the wall, and telling me how important it was. He kept saying I had to remember," Lucy told them, smiling as she remembered the dream.

"And so you did," her mother said wonderingly.

"That's very impressive, my dear," her father added.

"It was important to him," John continued. "I wonder what other secrets are hidden in that building?" he pondered.

"We'll just have to wait and see what else turns up," Lucy said with a shrug, then a smile as she remembered her parents were on the other end of a phone call and couldn't see her.

"Well, honey, I am very impressed," Rita said. "I can't believe you found it!" she added again.

"I can," John said. "I knew you would do it. You would never let Alba slip away like that, especially not to a Ricci," he said confidently. "When I gave you Alba, I trusted you to keep it in the family, and now you've proven that you'll do whatever it takes. I'm proud of you, Luce," he added, his voice warm.

"Thank you, Dad," Lucy said, her heart swelling. "And thanks for all your help with this," she continued.

"Nonsense, honey," Rita cut her off. "That's what parents are for!"

"Well, I'll let you go," Lucy said. "I just wanted to let you know that everything is taken care of."

"Thank you, sweetie," John said into the phone. "We have to head over and pick up your grandparents," he added. "We're taking them to all-day bingo!" he exclaimed, voice dripping with false enthusiasm. "We love you!" both her parents called into the phone, before resuming their debate about the phone, this time about how to hang up.

"Love you too!" Lucy called back before hanging up the phone, solving the problem for them.

"Well, what now, kitty cat?" Lucy asked the kitten, who was still sitting next to her.

*I should go grocery shopping,* Lucy realized. *Charlie will be here tomorrow, and there is pretty much no food in this apartment.*

With a sigh, Lucy pushed herself up from the couch. *It was nice enough out this morning,* she thought. *I'll skip the jacket.* Slipping on her shoes, she headed out the door and down the street to the corner store.

# Chapter 12

"He threatened you?!" Charlie exclaimed the next evening, sitting in one of the bar stools at Lucy's counter. "I can arrest him for that!" he declared. It was Monday night, and they were finally having their second date in Lucy's apartment.

"No, no," Lucy placated. "I mean, he did threaten me, but he doesn't need to be arrested. I think he's scared enough as it is," she said, with a smile, serving the pasta she had prepared into two large bowls.

"Fine," Charlie conceded. "But if he ever says another word to you, you let me know," he said firmly, pointing a finger at Lucy. "But, beside the point, I'm much more interested in that delicious-smelling dish you have there," he said, with an appreciative sniff.

"Have you had pasta carbonara before?" Lucy asked, bringing the bowls to the counter and setting them down. She came around the counter to sit down, removing her apron to reveal the light blue dress she and Ally had carefully picked out - from Ally's closet. Lucy didn't have many options for a date.

"Of course!" Charlie said. "Never prepared by a true Italian chef, though," he added, taking a sip of his wine as Lucy came around the counter.

"I'm no chef," she said. "I do know how to make a mean bowl of pasta, though!" she joked as she sat down. She picked up her glass and clinked it against Charlie's. "To second chances," she toasted.

"To second chances," he repeated, before they both took sips, their eyes connecting over the rims.

"So, you really found the bill of sale? And it's over, just like that?" he asked, setting his glass back down on the counter.

"I think so. I mean, I have the proof that I needed," Lucy replied with a shrug, picking up her fork. "I'm going to send it over to a lawyer, a friend of Ally's, just in case, but I think that Lucas has figured out he won't win. At least not this battle," Lucy continued, twirling the first bite of pasta around her fork. Charlie was about to take his first bite; she paused, waiting to see what his reaction would be.

"Delicious!" he declared after swallowing. "The best carbonara I've ever had. It's so creamy!" he raved, taking another bite.

"It's my nonno's recipe," Lucy told him. "The secret is the eggs. Most people use whole eggs, but he used whole eggs and extra egg yolks. It adds a little more richness and creaminess to the sauce," she explained. "It's one of my favorite meals," she confessed before finally taking a bite. The delicious, creamy sauce, flavored with smoked pork and pecorino cheese, had always been one of her favorite dishes. It was one her nonno had made for her all the time when she was young.

"No wonder. It's incredible!" Charlie declared.

They finished the meal, making small talk about Charlie's recent misadventures on the police force. He had been forced to pursue a suspect onto a playground earlier in the week, giving the playing children and their parents quite the scare.

"Hey, do you think there's anything else hidden in the cellar?" Charlie asked suddenly. "If he hid one important thing there, who's to say he didn't hide another?"

"Well, we didn't check," Lucy admitted. "I guess we were just so excited about the bill of sale we didn't think about it," she added.

"You probably should," Charlie suggested. "If he thought it was important enough for that, he may have put other important things there too."

"Well, do you want to go check right now?" Lucy asked, scooping up the last bit of her pasta.

"Now?" Charlie asked in surprise. "Sure, why not?" he said with a shrug. He collected the dirty dishes and deposited them in the sink. "I'll wash those when we come back upstairs, don't worry," he said with a smile.

"Charlie, you absolutely do not need to do the dishes. I invited you here; I'll wash them!" Lucy protested. "But let's go," she continued excitedly. "Do you really think Nonno hid something else down there?"

"Let's find out," Charlie said, grinning. With that, they both slipped on their shoes and hurried down the stairs to the restaurant door. Charlie jittered impatiently while Lucy fumbled with the key. On a Monday night, the kitchen was dark and quiet, totally empty except for Lucy and Charlie.

Finally, the door swung open and they both headed inside, Lucy pausing to click the door shut behind them. *Won't take any chances of anyone sneaking in behind us this time,* she thought to herself. She led the way to the cellar stairs and flipped on the light.

"Here we are," she said. "We found the bill of sale right there," she said, gesturing. "The brick didn't have any mortar around it," she added.

"Well, let's get to looking!" Charlie said. Together, they started examining the wall.

"Is that what it looked like?" Charlie asked, pointing to a spot about halfway down the staircase. It was another loose brick with no mortar around it. This one was easier to remove; it slipped right out of the wall in Lucy's hand.

"There's nothing back there," Lucy said, peering into the hole left in the wall. "Take a look," she said, stepping aside.

"No, no, look at the brick itself," Charlie told her, gently touching her arm. Lucy finally glanced down and saw that in the back of the brick, a tiny hole had been carved out, and something wrapped in white fabric was stuffed inside.

"Oh," Lucy commented in surprise. She sat down on the stairs, Charlie taking a seat next to her. She carefully pried the little bundle from the back of the brick, unwrapping it to reveal a golden charm.

"What is it?" Charlie questioned, his brow wrinkling as he peered at the charm resting in Lucy's hand.

"I think...I think it's a horn. A *corno*, in Italian. It's a good luck charm. It's supposed to protect from the evil eye," Lucy said slowly, as she turned the charm over in her hand. "He must have hidden this here as well."

"He must have left it here for us, to give the restaurant good luck" Lucy continued. "I know my mother wore a corno on her wedding day, and so did my grandmother, back in Italy. I wonder if this is the same one," she said thoughtfully, turning the charm over in her hand before offering it to Charlie.

"No, that's for you," Charlie said gently, closing Lucy's hand around the golden horn as he put his arm around her. "Are you going to keep it?" he asked.

"I'm going to put it right back where I found it," Lucy said decisively. "It's clearly working for us, and I'm not going to change a thing about it!"

"I think that's a very good idea," Charlie said, squeezing her closer. Suddenly, he leaned forward and planted a kiss on her cheek, almost on her nose. "Sorry," he apologized, leaning away.

Without replying, Lucy leaned forward and kissed him on the lips. "No apologies necessary," she said with a smile.

She carefully rewrapped the little charm and inserted it back into the brick. Together, she and Charlie slipped the brick, still holding it's precious cargo, back into the wall and headed up the stairs.

Reaching the apartment, they both sat on the couch. "Thanks for suggesting that we go take another look," Lucy said gratefully. "I wouldn't have thought of it myself."

"Hey, I *am* a police officer!" Charlie said with a smile. "I'm happy to have been able to help."

"Now then," he continued. "What exactly is the story with this little guy?" he asked, reaching out to scratch the kitten, who had jumped up between them. The cat responded with an appreciative purr.

"I found him out in the alley. He was all alone under the stairs. I was trying to find someone who would take him off my hands, but, honestly, at this point, I think I've gotten used to him," Lucy confessed.

"Does he have a name?" Charlie asked.

"Not yet. I haven't really thought about it." Lucy replied.

"When I was little, I used to have a stuffed animal that was a brown tabby cat, just like him. I called it Moose. Why, I have no idea!" Charlie said, laughing. "Maybe I was just confused about what a moose actually was."

"Moose," Lucy said, thinking it over while she fidgeted with her golden bracelet, a hand-me-down from her grandmother. "I like it. Moose," she said again. The kitten picked up its head, looking right at her. "Well, I think it's decided," she laughed. "Welcome home, Moose." The kitten flopped over onto her lap and started purring.

"I think he likes it," Charlie said with a laugh, petting the kitten. Lucy leaned back against the couch, resting for a moment and appreciating the little bundle of happiness sitting on her lap.

After a moment, she sat back up. "Ready for dessert?" she asked Charlie.

"There's dessert too?" he asked in mock astonishment. "Listen, I am always ready for dessert," he said. "Literally, anytime, day or night," he continued, smiling.

"Well, good!" Lucy exclaimed, moving Moose from her lap to the couch and standing back up. "Ally made us something special. She may have gotten a little carried away," Lucy admitted. "She was excited."

"What did she have to be excited about?" Charlie asked as Lucy pulled Ally's beautiful fruit tart out the refrigerator and prepared to slice it.

"Well, I don't exactly go on a lot of dates," Lucy confessed. "Neither of us do. We spend too much time in the restaurant," she said with a shrug. "So when one of us does, it's big news," she continued, carrying two plates with big slices of the tart back to the couch. Ally had filled the homemade shortbread crust with creamy vanilla custard before topping it with fresh strawberries, blackberries, blueberries, kiwis and peach slices, all tossed in a fruit glaze that made them sparkle under the bright lights.

"Wow, she made this?" Charlie asked in awe as Lucy delivered the plates. "She sure did," Lucy said, sitting down. "Ally is really talented. We're very lucky to have her here," she said, pausing to take a bite. She smiled as the cool vanilla flavor filled her mouth, before quickly being overpowered with the bright flavors of the fresh fruit topping.

"This is delicious!" Charlie exclaimed. "But not as good as the pasta," he said quickly, smiling. "But I don't want to talk about Ally. Tell me more about yourself," he requested, taking another bite.

"I mean, you know a lot of it," Lucy said with a smile. "I was born here in Boston, and I've lived in this apartment since I was born. My grandparents retired from the business before I was even born, but they were still around until they passed away. They moved into a ground-level apartment a few blocks from here. My nonno died when I was about eight, and Nonna passed a few years later." Lucy paused to take a breath, and another bite of the delicious tart.

"I grew up here, went to Johnson & Wales, and then came back here. After a few more years, my parents retired and moved out west, to be with my other set of grandparents, and here I am," she finished, shrugging. "That's all there is to it."

"I still think it's so cool that this place has been in your family for three generations," Charlie marveled, looking around as he set his empty plate on the coffee table.

"Well, it's not too impressive." Lucy laughed. "The place is awfully small," she said.

"Well, that's certainly true," Charlie conceded jokingly, returning Lucy's smile.

"Now it's your turn," Lucy said. "Did you grow up around here?" she asked, getting up to refill their wine glasses.

"I was actually born in Atlanta, Georgia," he said with a smile.

"Really?" Lucy asked in astonishment.

"I know, I know," Charlie said. "No one ever pegs me for a southern boy. I did move up here when I was twelve, though," he continued.

"And why was that?" Lucy asked, returning to the couch.

"Well, my parents both passed away, in a car crash," he said, looking down into the glass of wine Lucy had just returned to him. "I came up here to live with my uncle, who basically raised me."

"Oh, Charlie, I'm so sorry," Lucy apologized. "I never should have asked."

"No, no, it was a long time ago," he said. "So, I moved in with my uncle, up in Revere, and he raised me. I joined the army after I graduated from high school, and then the police force after that. I still live up in Revere—but I have my own house now!" he added with a laugh.

"Hey, you're doing better than me," Lucy said with a grin. "I still live in my parents' place!" They both laughed.

With that, Charlie set down his glass of wine. "I'm sorry, but I think I have to get going," he apologized. "My shift starts at six tomorrow," he explained.

"Of course, of course," Lucy said. "I'm sorry to keep you out so late," she said, noticing that the clock hanging on the wall showed the time as close to midnight. *Wow,* she thought. *We've been talking for a lot longer than I realized.*

"Not at all," Charlie said. "I had a really great time, Lucy." He stood up and put on his jacket, standing nervously by the door. Lucy got up and joined him there, ready to lock up after he left. "I'm always careful after that break-in a few months ago," she told him with a smile.

"Good!" he declared. "Thanks for making dinner," he continued, reaching out and taking her hand.

"Of course. I had a really great time too, Charlie," Lucy said. "Thank you for coming,"

"I'll give you a call soon," Charlie said. "We can go out again, or maybe I can cook for you next time," he offered.

"Will you actually call?" Lucy asked skeptically.

"I promise," he said, squeezing her hand. With that, he opened the door and stepped out onto the balcony. "Have a good night," he said, disappearing down the stairs.

"You too," Lucy called out into the darkness.

# Chapter 13

The next morning, Lucy and Ally met in the dining room, bright and early. They had assembled all the memorabilia from the trunk in Lucy's apartment and were planning a new display for it right by the host stand, where people would be able to look while they waited for a table. Lucy had even included the picture of her teenaged grandparents, the one that had come all the way from Italy.

"Alright, here's what I've got," Ally said, dropping two bags on the table. She had offered to swing by the frame store on her way over to the restaurant and pick up supplies to get all the memorabilia neatly displayed.

"And this, too!" she announced, revealing that in her other hand, she carried a takeout tray from the coffee place at the end of the street. "You're the best!" Lucy cried, eagerly accepting the cup of coffee Ally offered.

"I know, I know," Ally replied, laughing. Together, they unpacked the frames and laid them out on the table. Arranging and rearranging the pictures and menus, they were finally able to agree on a final layout, Ally having spent the morning relentlessly teasing Lucy about her date the night before. They had just started to take the backs off of the frames when they were interrupted by a knock at the door.

"Who could that be?" Ally wondered out loud, squinting as she tried to see who it was through the pebbled glass in the doorway.

"I have no idea," Lucy responded. "It's not Lucas, that's for sure. I think he's afraid of us now. And clearly, he would have just barged in anyway," she said with a dry laugh.

Lucy crossed the restaurant to unlock the front door, curious about who it could be. She swung open the door to reveal an older woman, immaculately dressed, with a platinum bob.

"Andrea Anders!" Lucy said in surprise, recognizing the woman with the platinum bob who had left her business card the other night. "I'm sorry, we don't open for a few more hours," she said apologetically.

"Of course, dear, but that's not why I'm here," Andrea said confidently, stepping over the threshold. "You never called me. Why not?" she asked, moving her sunglasses to the top of her head. Ally crossed the room to join them.

"Well, frankly, Ms. Anders, I'm not interested in selling the building," Lucy said firmly. "But thank you for your interest," she continued politely. Suddenly, they were interrupted by the sound of a ringing phone.

"Shoot, I'm sorry!" Ally apologized, pulling her cell phone out of her pocket. She headed through the swinging door into the kitchen.

"Our executive chef, Alison Pope," Lucy said belatedly as they watched Ally disappear.

"Oh good, I'd like to speak to her as well. Lucy, I'm not interested in buying your building," Andrea explained, her voice patient. "I'm interested in you," she continued with a smile. "As you may know," she continued, "my husband and I own the Anders Restaurant Group. We own several restaurants in Beacon Hill and Back Bay," she said, naming two of the more exclusive neighborhoods in the city.

Taking a breath, she continued, "We feel that the next opportunity for Beacon Hill will be an authentic Italian restaurant, and we feel that it will be very lucrative. We mean to take advantage of the opportunity, and we want you on board," Andrea said with a smile.

"What?" Lucy said, her head spinning. "Me? What do you want me to do?" she asked, wrinkling her brow in confusion.

"After you passed our little test the other night, with Philip playing the rude customer, we decided that we want you to come work for us. We want you to open the restaurant and be the general manager," Andrea explained.

"No, no, I can't do that," Lucy protested. "What about Alba? I can't leave it. I would never," she said, shaking her head.

"I wish that wasn't the case, but I do understand. If my first option didn't work for you, how about this one?" Andrea continued. Lucy was dimly aware that Ally had reentered the dining room. Andrea spoke, offering, "What if we act as your financial backers, and open a second Alba location? Operating under the Anders umbrella, of course. We will invest in you, and you will be able to continue, operating both restaurants. After hiring some managers, of course."

Lucy felt even more confused. *A second Alba?* she thought to herself. "I-I need to think about this, Ms. Anders," she finally responded. "I need some time," she said.

"Of course, dear," Andrea replied with a smile. "I'll leave you to it. Please, feel free to call if you have any questions. Otherwise, I'll be in touch in a few days. You do still have my card, right?" she asked.

"Yes, of course...that is, I think so," Lucy stuttered. She had no idea where that business card had ended up.

"Here, have another," Andrea said, pressing one into Lucy's hand. "And one for Ms. Pope, as well," she said, nodding in Ally's direction and adding a second card to Lucy's hand. "Tell her congratulations from us at Anders. Have a wonderful day now, ladies," she said, striding through the front door back out into the sunlight.

"What just happened?" Ally called out, hurrying across the restaurant.

"I...I'm not really sure," Lucy admitted. "She wants to finance us to open a second location. Another restaurant. She and her husband own a restaurant group, I guess. They ate here the other night," she told Ally, showing her the business card.

"The Anders group?" Ally read. "I've actually heard of them. They own a lot of really good restaurants, Luce," she told her friend. "What are you going to do?" Ally asked, entwining her fingers.

"I told her I'd have to think about it, but I have no idea. No idea at all. Do you think we could handle a second restaurant? We can barely stay on top of things here," Lucy said, thinking out loud. "But I bet it would be a lot of fun," she added.

"It's kind of funny, actually," Lucy continued. "The whole time you've been waiting to hear about this award, I've been wishing there was one for restaurant owners," she admitted to her friend. "But really, this is kind of like getting an award, isn't it?"

Ally's face lit up in excitement. "Speaking of the award—that phone call, I'm a finalist! I'm a finalist for the Outstanding Young Chef award!" she exclaimed. "I'm going to Charleston in October for the award ceremony!"

"Ally, congratulations!" Lucy cried out. "I'm so, so, so proud of you!" she said, hugging her friend. "And listen, I really am sorry about the way I was acting. I was jealous, plain and simple," she continued. "But it was stupid. You deserve all the success in the world," she told her friend.

"Thank you," Ally said. "But that's so strange. How did she know that I'm one of the finalists?" Ally wondered. Suddenly, her expression changed as something clicked.

"She must have nominated me," Ally said slowly. "Or someone from Anders. I guess they would have told her that I was selected as a finalist," she continued.

"Oh my gosh," Lucy realized. "That makes total sense. Of course. They must have been interested in us for a while, not just since the other night," Lucy added thoughtfully. "If we do decide to open another restaurant, having an Outstanding Young Chef nominee - or winner - would certainly be good for their business."

"I guess we're better at this whole restaurant thing than we thought!" Ally said, linking her arm through Lucy's and guiding her back to their makeshift workstation. "Soon, everybody will want a Moretti-Pope restaurant on their block!" she declared with a grin.

## THE END

Read the next North End Mystery, out in August 2020!

# HEIST ON THE HARBOR

Lucy Moretti and her best friend, Ally Pope, are hard at work getting ready to open their next restaurant, Corno, with their new business partners, Philip and Andrea Anders. When the couple offers them a celebratory night out on a harbor cruise, it's hard to say no! But once on board, they find that a group of thieves have different plans. In addition to stealing their valuables, one of the thieves took a shot at the boat's captain, murdering him in cold blood before fleeing into the night.

Shaken after their traumatizing night at sea, Lucy and Ally vow to uncover the pirates and solve the murder, doubling down in their efforts as a new friend is accused of being involved. As work on Corno continues, Lucy finds herself distracted by the odd actions of her new boyfriend, Officer Charlie Fitz. Even after her precious cat, Moose, goes missing, Lucy is dedicated to the case. Will she and Ally be able to uncover the mastermind behind the daring heist?

# Ally and Lucy's Sweet Pea & Goat Cheese Stuffed Agnolotti

The perfect way to celebrate spring's arrival! Ally's recipe creates a bright, creamy filling with just a hint of spice. Stuffed into fresh pasta pouches, this meal is perfect for a cool spring evening. Pair with a light white wine for the perfect meal. Serves 4.

FOR THE PASTA:
- 4 large eggs
- 1 large egg yolk (using just the yolk makes for a richer pasta)
- 2 ½ cups 00 flour (00 flour - *dopio zero*, in Italian -  is a more refined grind of flour. It yields a softer, smoother dough that is easier to work with. If you can't find it, AP flour will work nearly as well)
- 1 tsp kosher salt

1. Create a "well" of flour on your clean countertop by forming the flour into a pile and gently using your fingers to create an opening in the center.
2. Add the eggs and salt to the well, using a fork to whisk. The eggs will pull flour away from the sides as they combine. When the center

mixture is too stiff to whisk, use your hands
to knead the rest of the flour into the dough.

3.  Continue kneading until the dough is smooth
    and elastic, around 5 minutes.

4.  Wrap the dough in plastic wrap and let it rest
    at room temperature while you make the
    filling.

FOR THE FILLING:
- ½ lb mild goat cheese
- 2 cups fresh peas, steamed
- ½ cup grated Pecorino Romano
- 1 cup mascarpone cheese
- 1 oz fresh sage leaves, chopped fine
- 1 tsp red pepper flakes
- 2 tsp salt
- 1 egg

1.  In a large bowl, combine all ingredients
    except for the egg. Stir using a wooden spoon
    or rubber spatula. Some of the peas will burst,
    turning the filling a pale green, but you want
    some to remain whole. Do not over mix.

2.  Taste the mixture and adjust seasoning if
    needed. Once you are happy with the flavor,
    stir in the egg. Mix just enough to combine.

Stuff the agnolotti (see Technique, below) and cook
in boiling, salted water. They should take 3–4
minutes to cook. Ally recommends topping with a
sauce made from butter allowed to melt and brown
on the stove for a few minutes over low heat. For

extra flavor, add a few sprigs of tarragon to the butter while it browns.

## TECHNIQUE: Agnolotti

Agnolotti are a stuffed pasta, similar to ravioli, but with an easier technique that forms a pillow shape. To make them, start by rolling out your pasta dough to approximately 1/16th of an inch thick, working with ¼ of the dough ball at a time. Keep the rest wrapped up so it remains moist and easy to work with. A good test is to hold a sheet of rolled-out dough up to the light—if you can see shadows behind it, it's thin enough. Form your dough into rectangles about 4 inches wide, and as long as you have room for.

With the long side of the dough rectangle facing you, spoon the filling onto the dough a little less than a tablespoon at a time. Space the little mounds out, about two inches apart, all the way down the long side of the dough. They should be positioned about 1 inch from the edge of the dough closest to you. Using a pastry brush, or your finger, to brush water around the filling. This will allow the pasta to create a better seal.

Fold the long edge of the pasta over the filling, forming a triangle shape over the filling. Roll the triangle forward one more time, sealing the filling inside and leaving unfilled pasta extending past the seal. Use your fingers to seal the spots between the agnolotti by pressing down firmly. Now cut them apart, using either a knife or pastry cutter, if you have one. Trim off any excess pasta from the sealed edges, leaving about ½ inch of unfilled pasta extending past the seals.

Now, enjoy! You can cook the agnolotti right away or freeze them to enjoy later. Serve with your choice of sauce, although they are traditionally served with light sauces so as to let the flavor of the filling shine.

# ABOUT THE AUTHOR

Priscilla Baker lives in Boston, Massachusetts, with her partner and two cats. She works full-time in the restaurant industry and has finally found an outlet for all of her crazy stories—writing! She released her debut novel, *Murder at St. Mark's*, in the spring of 2020. When she's not writing, Priscilla enjoys reading, knitting and traveling.

Priscilla writes cozy mystery novels, combining her love of food and writing into one. Her North End Mysteries series focuses on Lucy Moretti, a young woman who has taken over her family's long-running Italian restaurant. The books take place in Boston's historic North End neighborhood, known for delicious food, Italian heritage and a dark past.

Visit Priscilla online at www.priscillabakerauthor.com.